WEREWOLF DREAMS

By: M.M. Anderson

DEDICATION:

For my brave, brilliant, beloved father,
James F. O'Sullivan, and the kid's last fight.
Gone but never forgotten.

Blue Moon

Blue Moon, you saw me standing alone,
Without a dream in my heart,
Without a love of my own,
Blue moon, you knew just what I was there for,
You heard me saying a prayer for,
Someone I could care for,

And then there suddenly appeared before me,
Someone my arms could really hold,
I heard you whisper "Darling please adore me,"
And when I looked to the moon it had turned to gold,

Blue moon, now I'm no longer alone,
Without a dream in my heart,
Without a love of my own.

Rodgers & Hart

Chapter 1

PARK PATROL

The moon was a waxing crescent.

Officer Seamus Sullivan, New City's lone werewolf policeman, slurped the raspberry jelly out of a Krinkle Kreme donut and lobbed the frosted dough lump out the window of his blue and white patrol car. It bounced off the rim of an overflowing garbage can and landed in the paws of a ragged rat. Feeding Midtown Gardens residents wasn't the same as littering, not in Seamus's mind, anyway.

"Park patrol," Seamus groaned as he reached for a cruller. An insatiable sweet tooth and wet dog body odor were constant but bearable human-form werewolf traits, although soggy canine funk insured that Seamus's love life remained nonexistent. Also on the downside list of werewolf traits was the "never age" dilemma, which meant Seamus would stay seventeen forever. On the *totally* downside of werewolf was the "moon" matter, and as Seamus had learned, the "controlling your anger" problem. Both of these occurrences made him sprout coarse black fur and razor-sharp incisors, which led to the "holy smokes" response that prompted Sergeant Gaffney to consult a lunar calendar and give Seamus blue moon vacation time and full moon days off.

After a recent newspaper article appeared, the sergeant also saw to it that Seamus was assigned solo nightshift park duty, until further notice. Midtown Gardens was closed to the public from 10:00 PM to 6:00 AM. Seamus and his New City Police

Department radio car were posted to make certain the park stayed vacant and graffiti-free.

"Sarge, what am I? A watch dog?" Seamus protested when he heard about his new patrol detail.

Sgt. Gaffney didn't respond, or look up from his desk blotter. The reassignment wasn't open for discussion. Despite being annoyed and having a bruised ego, Seamus decided he wouldn't push the park patrol issue. He knew Sergeant Gaffney had no choice but to protect his own twilight career and Seamus's hairy butt from controversy and scrutiny, or worse.

Midtown Gardens duty notwithstanding, Seamus also knew there was a definite upside to being an undead werewolf—still living.

Seamus possessed an overzealous fight gene and never retreated when danger reared its homicidal head. In his four years as an officer of the law, Seamus would have died many violent deaths had he still been a mortal. On duty and off, Seamus hated bullies. They made him react, and more often than not, lose his Irish temper. On the offensive, Officer Sullivan experienced first-hand what it was like to be stabbed, shot, bludgeoned, electrocuted, squashed by a renegade train, pushed off a bridge, and blown-up in a fiery skyscraper terrorist attack. He walked away unscathed (usually on all fours) from each altercation.

Eternal life undead had earned Seamus a slew of medals for honor and valor, but it had also won him the unwanted attention of Lyman Newlin, famous has-been, trying to make a come-back,

New City Chronicle police reporter. The following editorial by Newlin appeared just prior to Seamus's park patrol reassignment:

Officer Seamus Sullivan from the 20th Precinct seems to rise from the ashes time and time again, like the mythical Phoenix. How does this young patrolman defy death? Can survival be attributed to a lucky break? And what about the mysterious black hound that seems to follow him around? Is Seamus Sullivan New City's very own superhero with a canine sidekick?

The buried-on-page-nineteen blurb went unnoticed by most New Citiers. Father X. Francis Benedict, however, read the piece with rapt interest.

Mickey Stella, wanna-be wise guy, two-time jailbird, part-time hit man, and small-time stolen goods fencer sat alone at the end of the Cock of the Flock Tavern bar. He puffed an unfiltered cigarette and nursed his fifth and final bottom-shelf double Scotch & soda. He'd been cut-off by the bartender for uninhibited off-gassing.

Mickey was low on cash and irritated about being stood up by some guy who was going to cut him in on some sort of great deal, moving stuff from an electronics heist. Something to do with eye pads or pea pods. The alcohol had made Mickey's recall more foggy than usual. Not to mention years of hallucinogenic drugs, lack of exercise, and a diet high in GMOs and partially hydrogenated oils.

Mickey liked to think of himself as a big guy, the bouncer type. Mickey had horizontal butt crack on the back of his neck and could no longer bet numbers higher than ten. Most people who knew Mickey referred to him as a dumb, fat mook—even his Catholic mother.

Mickey knew this for certain because he used to go with her to church.

Mama Stella lit devotional candles and prayed for her only child every morning at 7:30 mass, "Dear Holy Mary Mother of God, please watch over my dumb, fat mook son and forgive me for whatever trespasses I did wrong to give birth to such a loser. Amen."

Mickey stumbled out of the Cock of the Flock Tavern and squinted at his watch dial. It was either 12:10 or 2:00. He couldn't quite tell, but he was coherent enough to know he had a transportation issue. Mickey hadn't considered finding a lift home, and he refused to take the bus or subway, not at this late hour anyway, all the weirdoes, too scary.

Mickey expected the guy with the goods to have wheels and drive him back over the bridge to Sicily Town after their deal went down. Mickey had planned to choke the guy lifeless, bury the body, and keep the car for a few days. Mickey's Caddie was in the shop again and Mama Stella wasn't exactly generous with her antique Pacer. The moon buggy sported a bumper sticker that read: HIT ME AND WE EXPLODE TOGETHER.

That was Plan A. Mickey didn't have a Plan B, and he didn't have return cab fare to Sicily Town. Not that any New City taxi driver would have ferried Mickey over the bridge to Sicily

Town, not at such a late hour, for any price, all the weirdoes, too scary.

With drunken clarity, Mickey decided to walk the six and a quarter miles back to his basement apartment, the studio he rented from his mother. Mickey hoped she wasn't waiting up, although he knew she would be. He pictured her sour face glued to the kitchen window next to the cellar door, waiting, watching, worrying. Mama Stella wouldn't let Mickey go to sleep without first giving her a detailed account of his evening. Mickey had long ago run out of credible fibs for his many midnight escapades, especially fibs to explain all the digging that went on in the vegetable garden after dark.

Four short blocks later, Mickey was bathed in sweat and there was a raw spot on his inner butt cheek where his size 48 briefs had crawled and bunched and began chafing. "This freakin' sucks!" Mickey screamed to no one as he dislodged the wedgie. A few slow steps later the wilted traveler removed his sports jacket, and unbuttoned his damp rayon dress shirt collar before cursing the heat, which now topped the list of Mickey's mounting aggravations.

Middle of the night and the mercury was still hovering around a humid 85 degrees. Tomorrow snow was in the forecast—that was springtime in New City.

A lone cab stopped for the light. Mickey ambled forward and grabbed the passenger door handle, but not before the driver caught sight of the Neanderthal would-be fare in the rearview mirror, pushed auto-lock, and sped away. Mickey tumbled onto the curb. It wasn't his night.

"Eat dung! You diaper head, camel face, toilet… freakin'… mother… ah, shit!" Mickey's voice was hoarse from too many smokes and chronic post-nasal drip. He now had a rip in his sleeve and his elbow was scuffed. He sat on the grimy concrete for a moment and tried his best to contemplate the situation. The park loomed in front of Mickey's weary view. If he wanted to get home any time before dawn he'd have to pick himself up and continue walking.

Mickey decided Plan B was to skim a mile or so off his impossible foot journey by cutting through Midtown Gardens.

Mickey crossed the street and yanked the CLOSED sign from the park's entryway gate, bent it in half, tossed it into the deserted avenue, and wished aloud in a flurry of expletives that the discarded metal would tear through the next passing cab's tire.

Two hundred yards away, the clink-clank-clinking of aluminum sign on potholed asphalt awoke Seamus from a momentary snooze. The scent of sour body odor, blood, tobacco, and cheap booze also reached Seamus long before Mickey lumbered through the park clearing. The trespasser stopped beside a lonely bench where he paused to pee on an over-flowing garbage can. Seamus walked up behind Mickey, flashlight in hand.

"Let's go, Chief," Seamus said.

Mickey jumped. "What the—?"

"Park's closed. Or didn't you read the sign before flinging it into the street?"

Mickey finished urinating in silence, shook twice, then pushed his pecker back into his fly and wiped a wet hand on his pant leg.

"Prove I flinged the sign onto Garden Avenue, flatfoot. Smells like a stinkin'wet dog around here." Mickey sniffed his own armpits.

"Emptied your tank, now beat it. If you wanna tip-toe through the tulips, come back after 6:00." Seamus motioned with the flashlight beam, illuminating the direction of nearest park exit. "Start walking."

Mickey sat himself down on a park bench next to the garbage can. "I ain't going nowheres, flatfoot."

According to the Police Handbook Course of Action, Section 10, when dealing with an intoxicated person an officer should:

1. Establish contact in a friendly manner and gain trust.

2. Never be condescending.

3. Don't debate.

4. Blame the reason why the person has to leave on someone besides you.

5. Lie if you have to, to make them happy.

Seamus sighed. He hated dealing with drunks. The five rules of law enforcement procedure never seemed to work. He gave it a go anyway.

"Listen, Chief; it doesn't look like you had such a good night, but I don't make the rules around here. Go home. Things'll be better in the morning."

Mickey didn't move or reply.

"The park is closed—you gotta leave."

"Who says, flatfoot?" Mickey cocked his head and glared at Seamus.

"I says." Seamus folded his arms and stood erect, positioned cop-style steadfast in a puddle of lamppost light. Broad shouldered, muscular, 5'10", clean-cut, baby-faced, Seamus didn't look a day older than his forever seventeen years.

Mickey grinned.

In one fast and fluid motion, Mickey grabbed the nearby trashcan and crashed it across Seamus's knees.

Seamus collapsed like a house of cards on a windy day.

Mickey followed with a second crushing blow to the downed officer's head, splitting it like a ripe watermelon. Mickey rolled the bloodied policeman onto his back and helped himself to the vehicle keys before removing Seamus's service revolver from its holster. He fired two shots into the unconscious officer's chest, stuffed the smoking gun into his own waistband, and trotted towards the radio car.

Seamus's lupus conversion was swift and furious.

Mickey made it twenty yards across the clearing before he heard the pursuing patter of paws. The cop killer slowed his lumbering jog and glanced over his left shoulder. He was eye-to-eye with a furious frothing werewolf.

"Big dog!" yelled Mickey, pulling the revolver from his waistband. He didn't get the opportunity to fire. An enormous pair of razor-sharp jaws clamped over Mickey's fleshy neck with the force and speed of a guillotine. He was DOA before his decapitated corpse hit the grass with a THUD.

By the time the frenzied werewolf had consumed Mickey's cirrhosis liver, not a trace of desecrated carcass remained. It had burst into a momentary flame and vanished into the darkness. Whatever personal articles were left behind comprised a pile of soon-to-be-windblown ashes.

Except the gun. It belonged to Seamus.

Seamus the werewolf loped back towards the patrol car, his rage subsiding along with his consciousness. His stomach was already beginning to boil and cramp. *Don't eat drunks' livers.*

Seamus heaved and drooled and retched and hurled Mickey chunks before catching sight of the familiar apparition hovering above the grass. There she was again, watching him from her glistening sphere of luminescence.

Seamus wagged his bushy black tail and whimpered an affectionate greeting. He liked it when phantom woman showed up to his kills in the buff. Tonight, however, she was wearing pink paisley pajamas. All the same, nude or clothed, she was hot.

It wasn't long before Seamus's vision faded to black.

Lights out.

Chapter 2

NOT SO SWEET DREAMS

Claudia awoke with a start. She canvassed the shadowy darkness for any sign that the dream wolf had accompanied her back to abrupt consciousness. Everything was where it should be. Save for her snoring cat, Misha, the room was quiet and still. The digital clock on the nightstand glowed, 2:27 AM. Claudia sat up and adjusted the skewed silky bodice of her pink paisley pajamas. She needed a drink of water.

Claudia approached the kitchen at the opposite end of the apartment. She could sense the metaphysical energy of two dead persons. Claudia considered skipping bottled water in favor of bathroom tap, but it was too late. Her name was being called.

Los padres.

Claudia could tell from the vibes that her parents were quarreling. Probably about her brother, Alex. She tried to hum a shielding tune while grabbing a water from the fridge. No luck. Two animated dialogues crashed into Claudia's brain at once. The dead don't speak—they send, like an high-priority email. Claudia had to strain to process it all. She wasn't in a medium mood.

"Shhhh, *por favor*. It's the middle of the night," Claudia replied. "Don't worry so much about Alex. He's a big boy." Claudia preferred to speak aloud to the departed. Although they could hear her thoughts, she found the mind reading disconcerting.

These days Salvador and Paz limited their visits to the kitchen. They hadn't always been considerate. Claudia's parents spent most nights after the accident in their daughter's room, hovering, crying, arguing. It just about drove Claudia batty.

Fortunately, the midnight appearances became less frequent over the years. Once Claudia erupted into puberty and began sleeping in the buff, Salvador and Paz Peña kept clear of her bedroom, most of the time. When they floated in on their son and a rambunctious cheerleader engaged in primal gymnastics on the game room pool table, *los padres* began congregating in the kitchen. There was no sex and nudity in the kitchen. Not yet, anyway.

Claudia heard her brother's key in the front door.

Los padres departed.

Alex poked his head into the kitchen. "Why are you still up?"

"I'm not 'still up'. I was asleep a few minutes ago." Claudia yawned.

"*Lobo sueño?*"

"Yes, a really revolting dream, wolf decapitated a big fat guy, ate his liver and then puked bloody chunks."

"Hmm, thanks for the visual." Alex grimaced. "Glad I ate dinner hours ago."

"It's been a while since my last dream."

"That's good news."

"Wolf was very excited to see me. He wagged his tail and howled, like a big, happy puppy." Claudia took another sip of water.

15

"The wolf has a thing for you. See his doggie erection again?"

"Alex!" Claudia screamed. "I should have never told you that!"

"Your dream descriptions are pretty vivid, Sis. Happy to report that I wake up with no sleepy-time memories, and that's the way I like it."

"I know. There's something very real about these nightmares." Claudia finished her water. "Sounds weird, but I sort of enjoy them."

Alex was still standing in the kitchen doorway. "You are weird. And, speaking of really weird, are we alone?"

"Yes. It's safe to enter. Mami and Papi left when you came home, but not before I had to listen to tonight's squabble—about you," Claudia pointed her finger at Alex.

"Me? Favorite son?"

"Mami says she doesn't approve of you throwing money away in a nudie club after the game, and Papi says you swung late. That's why you flew out in the 4th."

Alex's olive complexion turned pink. "Mami went inside the club?"

"Papi wanted to go too but Mami made him wait in the parking lot. They were bickering about it when I came in here to get a water."

"I would've drunk out of the toilet bowl to avoid that argument." Alex shuddered.

"Why are you loitering in a titty bar, anyway? We haven't lived in this concrete jungle two months and already half the supermodels in New City have left you 'pick me' messages on our answering machine."

"It's my first season—just trying to fit in with the guys." Alex shifted his eyes away from his sister's perceptive stare.

"If you say so." Claudia knew the truth, thanks to her parents' detailed account of Alex's post-game activities. Despite a *flaca* flock of female aficionadas, Alex had the hots for a very tall, bodacious stripper. It was his idea, not the guys, to return to the same gentleman's club for the third night in a row.

"Did Mami and Papi see my game-winning homer?" Alex changed the subject.

"Don't know. But I do know you'd better hope the paparazzi didn't see you go into Angel Alley. Let me think of a catchy People Page headline…"

"Mami and Papi told you the name of the place?

"Yep, and a whole lot more. Can't keep your eyes and money off Violet the purple-haired pole dancer. Can she really lick her own belly-button?" Claudia stuck out her tongue.

"Hey, now that boarders on tattling." Alex grabbed a container of milk from the refrigerator, gulped it down, and let out a loud belch.

"Alejandro! Disgusting!" Claudia scolded. "Don't try changing the subject. Yuck, now the milk has back wash."

"Spit-free." He turned the jug upside down. "See? Empty."

"You're dribbling onto the floor."

"Call the cat. Pssst, here Misha, Misha."

"She's sleeping."

Alex grabbed a dish towel and threw it over the drips. He proceeded to mop with his foot. "Only because Misha isn't eating."

"Don't make fun of my chubby, lazy cat and use a paper towel to wipe the floor."

Alex pitched the towel into the sink and took a seat at the table. "*Los padres* floating to the Bean Town series?"

"*No sé.*" Claudia shrugged. "I was recovering from a nightmare guts-munching, remember?"

"And wolf vomiting. How could I forget? Ask your poltergeist pals to explain why you've been having gory nightmares."

"I don't talk to dead people," Claudia corrected him. "They talk to me. I've asked *los padres* about my dreams. Papi smiles and Mami frowns."

"Ah, mixed reviews. This has been going on for what, five years?"

"Since I was 12 and played that haunted sleepover game," Claudia reminded him. "You were on the road and I stayed with your friend's family."

Alex replied in a slow spooky Halloween narrator voice. "Oooo, Mary Worth, who silly girl legend has it, was brutally murdered on the eve of her wedding. Mary's heartbroken spirit roams the earth looking for her true love, and if her spirit is hokey-pokey summoned, Mary will reveal the face of her summoner's true love. Eerie… Creepy…Scary…"

18

"If it's just a silly legend then why when I walked backwards, in the dark, down the stairs, holding a candle and a mirror, chanting 'I believe in Mary Worth. Face of my beloved in the mirror come forth,' how come I saw a wolf?"

"The more puzzling question is: How come you didn't fall down the steps and break your neck?"

"Ha-ha, very funny." Claudia smiled. "If I saw the wolf, and the game is true, and it is true because I saw the wolf, then that means the wolf is my true love."

"Perfect logic." Alex rolled his eyes. "I'll marry a stripper and you'll marry a wolf. Miami and Papi will be so proud. Not. They'll haunt us forever."

"Why would I fall in love with a killer dream wolf?" Claudia wondered aloud. "Even if he does have the most amazing green eyes." Claudia omitted the fact that tonight's dream was more vivid than any of her many others, as if she were somehow closer to the wolf than she'd ever been before. "Maybe I need a boyfriend."

"Maybe you don't need a boyfriend until you turn 18, or 30" Alex said, giving his sister a wink. "Maybe the wolf is symbolic. It means you love dreaming about wolves, because wolves are like dogs, and dogs are better pets than cats, because cats, I won't name names, because an unidentified white and black fluffy cat pees in my gym bag whenever I return home from a road trip."

"Misha misses you," Claudia defended her feline.

"Maybe your nightmares will end if I adopt a dog that misses you?" And eats your shoes if you go over your credit limit while shopping."

"You could get a big shoe-eating dog if we still lived in a house and had a yard," Claudia countered.

"I know you miss our old place, Sis, but you have to admit this is one amazing apartment, a penthouse overlooking New City's most famous park." Alex burst into song. "If I can make it there, I'll make it anywhere. It's up to you New—"

Claudia interrupted. "You did the hard sell already, before you signed your gazillion dollar contract: the shopping, theaters, museums, restaurants."

"And your horse is right across the street in Midtown Gardens' stables. No more manure aroma wafting through my bedroom window." Alex took a deep breath.

Claudia lobbed the bottle cap at her brother. "I liked it better when Pirate lived in our barn and you played for the Tampa Bay Pirates. Maybe you'll get traded back to warm sunny Florida."

"Pretty sure I'll be here for the extent of my Bombers' contract, unless I get hurt or forget how to whack a curve ball." Alex took a ball-less, bat-less swing.

"Papi won't let you forget," Claudia assured him.

"True."

"Hey, I have the mayor's charity dinner coming up," Claudia reminded.

"Who'd you choose to receive the scholarship money?" Alex asked.

"Saint something." Claudia shrugged. "Can't remember the school's odd name."

"Maybe the president of my foundation should have a better memory?"

"You can't replace me—I'm family. Besides, when I finish my secondary home schooling requirements, and go off to college, I'll need a well-paying flexible job that fits my hectic scholarly schedule." Claudia tossed her hair for emphasis. "A job worthy of my brains and unique talents."

"Looking beautiful, dressing well, choosing scholarship recipients, and speaking at honorariums." Alex provided Claudia's present job description.

"Exactly. Anyway, I just remembered the strange name of the school. I picked St. Guinefort's Home for Orphaned and Troubled Boys."

"Unusual French name."

"Even stranger, St. Guinefort was a dog who fought the devil, and won."

"So Guinefort is a saintly dog with a boys' school named after him? I trust your choice," Alex said. "You have good instincts."

"Hope so. No other school applied for the scholarship. I placed a dozen ads and mailed a hundred letters to schools across the city."

"That's weird."

"Yeah, I thought so, too." Claudia smiled. "Slight change of subject, since I don't have a boyfriend, I need an escort for the dinner."

"Have you made any friends your age at the stable?" Alex asked.

"No. Horses owned by middle-aged mistresses, for the most part. I don't really fit in, so I keep to myself." Claudia added. "Heard they call me the Lone Ranger."

"Ask Freddy the doorman to be your date; if he says 'yes', buy him some dentures." Alex folded his lips over his teeth.

"You're bad, Alex. Freddy is sweet, but not my century. Any cute single guys on the team you can fix me up with?"

"I told you, we're on the road that weekend." Alex stood and threw the milk jug into the recycle bin. "Two points!"

"What about that rookie short stop with the muscles and Mohawk? He's on the DL. He can skip the game and go to the dinner with me."

Alex helped himself to a green apple from the fruit bowl. "Nope. Ballplayers are bad news."

"Not all. Refrigerator etiquette and stripper fetishes aside, you're pretty awesome, big brother."

"Glad you see my finer qualities," he mumbled through a mouth full.

"Mami and Papi are very proud of you."

"Beloved son."

"And you're my hero," Claudia teased, but wasn't kidding.

"You want a new dress for the dinner?"

"Already bought one, off the runway. Charged it to your black card." Claudia yawned when she caught a glimpse of the kitchen clock. "Wow, it's almost 3:00. I'd better get back to bed if I'm going to take Pirate for an early morning ride. Park and stable open at 6:00. My plan is to ride at dawn."

"Knock yourself out. The team plane leaves at ten. Sure you don't want to spend the weekend in Bean Town?"

"Stop worrying about leaving me alone."

"Who's worried? It's just that we're new to town and you might get lonesome."

Claudia knew her brother well. "You'll be back after Sunday's double-header, right? I'll be fine here by myself for one night. This is the poshest neighborhood and building in all of New City."

"Still means you should be careful; stay home after dark and keep the door locked and the alarm activated."

"*No te preocúpe.* I also have Mami and Papi hovering around me, when they aren't hovering around you."

"Very true. They're worse worriers than I am." Alex smiled. "G'night, baby sister. I'll see you Sunday. "

Claudia blew her brother a kiss.

Claudia headed back to her room. Misha was in the same place on the bed, snoring. In an effort to let sleeping cats lie, and warm bodies chill, Claudia slipped beneath the cool, crisp, cotton bed sheets. She closed her eyes, gathered the duvet up to her nose, and looked forward to a few more hours of sleep, sweet dreams without the company of wolf or parents.

One out of two…

Chapter 3

LOS PADRES

Paz and Salvador waited for their daughter to doze off before floating into her bedroom. The Alex argument continued.

"Alex should have a wife by now, not hanging around bars looking at a—"

"Paz, there is no need for calling names," Salvador declared. "Perhaps she is a nice girl with a not so nice job? Violet *es muy* …" He caught his wife's stern glare. "She's very tall."

"Alex would not spend his nights watching Violet if we lived," Paz huffed.

"If we lived our children would make decisions for themselves *tambien*," Salvador reminded his wife. "Alex has taken care of his sister since our deaths and he has become a famous man we are proud of. Do you forget Alex gave up his college scholarship and entered the baseball draft early in order to become Claudia's guardian? It should not matter if Alex finds a dancer attractive."

Paz cracked a grin and nodded in agreement. "*Aye, bien.* You used to stare at me in that way too when we first met."

"*¡La verdad!* And I still do." Salvador winked at his wife.

Paz stroked her daughter's cheek. "*Buenas noche, mi'ja bonita*… My pretty daughter."

"We should tell her about the wolf," Salvador said, his tone again serious.

"No, the wolf should go away." Paz waved her hand. "We helped the orphans to receive the scholarship money. *Los lobos* are not Claudia's responsibility."

"It is not our choice," Salvador kissed his sleeping daughter on the forehead. "They will meet."

"No!*"* Paz yelled. Even after death, her emotions could not be contained.

Misha leapt off the bed and into the closet.

Claudia stirred.

"Shhh, Paz, *no se la despierte*." Salvador held his finger to his lips.

"I am not waking her. It was the cat, and this wolf *problema* is all your fault." Paz kept her voice to a loud whisper.

"Mine?" Salvador raised his eyebrows.

"*Sí*, Salvador," Paz scolded. "Claudia would not have gone to the party if we did not die. She would have been home with her mami and papi instead of living in California with Alex and sleeping at the house of people who are not her family."

"It would have happened another way. It was fate." Salvador held firm.

"We could have protected her." Paz would not allow the topic to drop.

"We protect her now," Salvador reminded.

"We are dead because of you." Paz floated to the other end of the room.

Her husband followed. "Paz, it was agreed long ago. There is no blame. *Era nuestro tiempo de salir*."

"It was not time to leave the children." Paz wiped a tear.

"*Mi amor*." Salvador hugged his wife. "It was our fate," he said. "We have gone back to the accident many times. Fate cannot be changed."

"The wolf and Claudia." Paz said. "*El mismo*. The same."

"We cannot change what is." Salvador looked up to the heavens.

"*Quiero volver*," Paz pleaded.

"You want to return again, to the accident?"

"*Sí*."

"Paz, we've gone back so many times." Salvador shook his head and let out an exasperated sigh.

"Once more," his wife begged.

"*Será el mismo*."

"And I think maybe it will be different." Paz smiled.

"*Bueno*," Salvador threw up his hands in defeat.

Paz grinned. "I think this time you will see the accident was your fault."

"*¡Vámanos, esposa!*" Salvador disappeared.

Paz followed.

Los padres' spirits sat on the railing of the Hallandale Beach Bridge watching their past selves in an idling speedboat below.

An oblivious fisherman baited his hook. Paz stepped through him. He shivered.

"*Mire ésto.*" Salvador removed a single ski from the boat's gear compartment.

"Where is the other?"

"Only one. Today I will learn to slalom," Salvador declared. He laid the ski down on the boat deck and slid his feet into the linear straps. Both feet secured, he tipped over and caught himself on the captain's chair.

"How are you going to ski when you cannot stand?" Paz teased.

"It will be more simple in the water." Salvador threw back his broad shoulders.

"*Más difícil,*" his wife disagreed. "In the water it is more difficult. You must have much strength in your legs to balance on one ski."

Salvador sucked in his forty-five-year-old mini-gut and flexed his muscular chest and biceps. "*Soy fuerte como un toro.*"

"*Terco como un burro.*" Paz was smiling.

"True, strong like a bull and stubborn like a burro," Salvador agreed.

Paz kissed her husband. "*Una combinación perfecta.*"

The captain turned the wheel over to his wife.

"I will be triumphant!" Salvador boasted. He checked his life vest, secured the towline, and jumped into the water. He fastened the new ski and signaled. "Ready!"

Paz double-checked her rearview mirrors and pushed the throttle forward.

Salvador stood on his first try and hung steady behind the speeding craft. It was during a wake-crossing jump attempt that he lost balance and wiped out.

"*¡Bueno!*" Paz clapped. "You did it!"

Salvador thrust his fist in the air and declared victory.

Paz circled around to pick him up. She drove within a boat length of her husband and shifted into reverse.

"*¡No! Maneja hacia adelante!*" Salvador screamed. "Don't reverse! Drive forward!" The revving blare of the outboard motor obscured Salvador's pleas.

Paz ran over her husband. After realizing what she'd done —the water turned red and he ceased yelling—Paz left the boat running and jumped in to save Salvador.

The propeller was still spinning. It minced Paz into gory bits too.

Claudia was at school running PE laps when her parents appeared on the track infield. They were mutilated and carved, hemorrhaging from numerous slice wounds. Salvador wore a single water ski and Paz held a tattered lifejacket.

A wave of terrified grief flooded Claudia's sleeping sixth sense. She awoke with a start from her second reoccurring nightmare.

Chapter 4

BREAKFAST

The stationhouse was quiet for a between-shift Saturday morning.

Ring. Ring. Ring. Ring…

The front desk officer didn't report until 8:00 AM. Sgt Gaffney put down his bent nail clippers, pressed the blinking red extension-light button, and answered the phone.

"20th, Sgt. Gaffney … Whoa, ma'am, slow… slower. I can't understand a word you're saying…Your child's missing… When did you last see him or her?" Sgt. Gaffney dug through his desk looking for a pen and pad. "You saw him last night around 7:30… He went out to meet a friend. Did you call the other child's mother?... You don't know the other child's mother… An Amber Alert, of course…Yes, I can tell, and you have every right to be upset. Let me get some information. Name?… Mickey Stella… Age?... Thirty-seven. Thirty-seven? Ma'am, you're son's not a child… Yes, I understand he's your child, but thirty-seven-year-old men have been known to stay out all night… No, this changes the procedure… Right, I can't sound an Amber Alert or send an officer out to look for your son… It doesn't matter if he's a big stupid mook… I understand your son said he'd be home by midnight… I know it's 6:30 in the morning… Maybe your son fell asleep at his girlfriend's… Ma'am, stop screaming… True, you can't file a missing person's report for another day and a half… Well, every other precinct in New City is saying the same thing because we all follow the same procedures… You have a right to phone the newspaper… I'm not sure if the *Chronicle* has a Lost People section… 6'1" and 320 lbs." Sgt. Gaffney continued scribbling notes, with an imaginary pen and invisible paper. "Right. If we hear anything, we'll call."

Gaffney hung up the receiver and returned to his fingernail trimming.

Seamus passed the sergeant's office on his way to the locker room.

"Quiet park night, Sullivan?" Sarge asked.

"Mostly quiet." Seamus's gait was sluggish. He'd inherited Mickey's hangover.

The Sarge waved him in. "You don't look so good. Come in here. Sit down."

"My breakfast didn't agree with me." Seamus held his queasy stomach and plopped into his boss's tattered swivel chair.

It was Sgt. Gaffney who appeared to be the more ailing. He hopped up from his chair and closed the office door. "Please tell me you had rotten eggs for breakfast."

"No eggs."

"Wild berries off a poisonous vine?"

"Sorry."

"Rabid squirrel?"

"Nope, but I could go for a candy bar if you have one."

"By any chance was your breakfast 6'1" and 320 lbs? Please tell me I'm wrong."

"Sounds about right."

"Holy smokes," Sgt. Gaffney moaned. "Holy smokes… What am I going to do with you, Seamus?"

"Hey, Sarge, he killed me first," Seamus defended.

"Funny." Gaffney wasn't laughing. "I'm sure it's possible Mickey Stella deserved to get eaten by a werewolf." The Sarge's scowling face turned bright red.

"How do you know the guy's name?" Seamus remained calm.

"I'm making an educated guess. Some mook mama's boy named Mickey Stella is AWOL. His mother just phoned to place a missing persons report, and she plans to call the newspaper." Sarge put his hand over his heart and paused for a moment.

"You OK, Sarge?"

"No! This means if Mickey doesn't show back up, it's only a matter of time before your friend Lyman Newlin comes poking around here again."

"Why would Lyman get involved? He's a police reporter," Seamus reminded his boss. "People go missing in New City every day. Most of them show up, eventually."

"Unless they happen to tick you off first!"Sergeant Gaffney yelled.

"That's not fair, Sarge. I was minding my own business."

"Trouble seems to find you, Seamus." The Sarge rubbed his shiny bald head. "Now what am I supposed to do?"

"Nothing. There's no connection to me. You know how it goes."

"Yes, Seamus, I know how it goes," Sgt. Gaffney grumbled. "When full moon or fury strikes, you fall on all fours, and faster than I can spell 'transmogrification' you're changed into a killing carnivorous canine."

"You make it sound like poetry, Sarge."

Gaffney wasn't amused. "Yeah? One of these days there's gonna be real trouble. Lyman mentioned the wolf, mentioned you, Seamus the wolf, in his article."

"He said dog, 'big, black dog'," Seamus corrected.

"Dog, wolf, what's the difference? It's only a matter of time before Lyman's observations and articles mean there's gonna be an investigation, and that would make for a bigger problem than you, and I, already got."

"How? Bodies disappear without a trace, and I change back into a man with no credible connection between the omitted person, a dog, a wolf, my superior officer, or me. Not even a tourist with a cell phone can prove a kill." Seamus flashed a cheesy grin. "The werewolf doesn't photograph."

"That 'invisible to cameras' thing is, is so… It gives me the creeps!" Sgt. Gaffney kissed his medal of St. Michael.

"No pictures, no bodies." Seamus placed his hands behind his neck and leaned back in the swivel chair.

"It's a lucky break for us that you turn dead bad guys into dust. But that doesn't mean no one's gonna be looking for a missing person and asking questions, asking me questions, like the call I just got from Mickey Stella's mother." Sgt. Gaffney took a stash of antacids out of his desk drawer and downed a handful. "Want some?" He offered the bottle to Seamus.

"Nah, I'm going to go for a run and try to sweat it out." Seamus stood up and stretched.

"Sweat what out? I'm afraid to ask."

"Mickey was a Scotch drinker," Seamus said. "You know liquor doesn't sit well on my stomach."

"And your eating people doesn't sit so good with me either," the Sarge snapped. "I have less than two years until I retire, Seamus, less than two years, exactly five hundred and sixty-seven days until I turn in my badge and my service revolver and start drawing a pension. I'm going to do my 30 years. Don't ruin it for me!"

"Sarge, Sarge, everything with this Mickey guy is gonna turn out OK," Seamus assured. "Watch, his mama's gonna call you later to say her son is back home, safe and sound, like a good little mook."

"Maybe so." Sergeant Gaffney relaxed a bit. "But what about the guy you did munch in the park last night? What about his mama or wife or kids or friends? What if they start looking?"

"They're not going to find anything. You worry too much."

"And you don't worry enough."

"Dead guys don't fret." Seamus chuckled.

"You're not dead." Sgt. Gaffney lowered his voice and leaned across his desk. "You're *undead*. If you were dead you would have had a nice funeral and I would have bought a big flower arrangement wreath thing, and cried boo-hoo, and watched the padre bury you. But you're still walking around because you're *undead*, and it's because of me there's a seventeen-year-old werewolf on the NCPD."

"My driver's license says I'm 22."

"Yeah, well, you haven't aged a day or matured one bit since that other werewolf left you undead. Why were you at a construction site in the middle of the night, anyway?"

Seamus never told Sergeant Gaffney he'd been partaking in a solitary death-defying version of the X Games just before being attacked. He avoided the question with a question. "How can I mature when I'm always sent off by myself?"

"But somehow you don't manage to stay by yourself," the Sarge countered. "Somehow, Seamus, you keep ending up the hero cop, earning medals, and getting your name in the paper."

"Maybe if I had a partner?"

"Yeah? Who would I partner you with? Dracula?"

Seamus howled. "That's pretty funny."

"Ha-ha, big joke… You're on solo park patrol until I retire. Then I'll move to Florida, buy a boat, and forget about hairy monsters and lunar calendars and full moons, and my bleeding ulcer. Get it?"

"Yeah, Sarge." Seamus got it.

Sgt. Gaffney hadn't just been covering werewolf tracks and watching out for Seamus since the attack. Long before that, Sarge was a dedicated volunteer who ran the sports program at his alma mater, St. Guinefort's Home for Orphaned and Troubled Boys. It was Sergeant Gaffney who introduced Seamus to boxing. Having a sport to channel his fight urge kept Seamus out of trouble during his turbulent teen years. Most of the time.

Seamus used to think he could thank the Sarge, pay him back by way of a successful career in the ring. He'd be middleweight champion of the world, and take his mentor, trainer, and friend along for the ride to glory, fame, and fortune.

But life didn't work out that way.

Undead eliminated Seamus's "Rocky" aspirations. A pugilist opponent can't punch a latent lupus and live to throw another blow.

In his first undead training session, Seamus devoured a sparring partner who was duly notorious for dirty play. Seamus was able to shake off a groin grilling, but a clutch chomp on the ear rendered him red and his opponent vanished, quite dead.

Sarge wasn't the event's only spectator at the gym that evening.

A freelance photographer shot stills of the kill before his heart gave out. An empty ring appeared on the developed film.

Werewolves don't make good boxers, but like every one else without a trust fund, they need a day job. It took a few weeks, but Sgt. Gaffney finally came to terms with his moral quandary. When isn't a killing a murder—when it's it's the result of a fight, and there's no corpse left behind. He persuaded Seamus to sit for the police exam.

Seamus passed on his first try and graduated from the police academy on the day he never turned 18.

"Hey, Seamus, you falling asleep with your eyes open?" the Sarge barked.

Seamus returned from his reverie.

Sgt. Gaffney tossed Seamus a granola bar and a handful of sugar packets. "Put some breakfast on your stomach and go for your park run before it snows, but don't jog on any pedestrian paths. Keep away from other people. Far, far away. Got it?"

"Sarge, do you know anyone who's more of a loner than me?" Seamus headed for the locker room.

Chapter 5

BREAKFAST, PART 2

Claudia hadn't slept a wink since her second nightmare.

She was showered and dressed and was ready to depart for Midtown Garden stables before the buzz sounded on her alarm clock. Claudia skipped breakfast; she wasn't keen on spending time in the kitchen with her parents again so soon.

"Good morning, Miss Peña. You're looking ready for a new day mighty early." Doorman Freddy tipped his hat and flashed Claudia a cheerful gummy grin. His three teeth were like an old picket fence that had warped and rotted and lost a few planks.

"Morning, Freddy." Claudia looked away and promised herself she'd never again forget to floss.

Freddy escorted the newest Tacoma tenant under the entrance awning. There wasn't a pedestrian or car in sight.

"The city is so peaceful this time of the day," Claudia observed.

"That's why I sing with the birdies at sunrise," Freddy crooned. "We can hear our own voices. Especially on weekends when there's no traffic."

Claudia smiled. "I should get up this early more often."

"It's a fine day for riding, if that's where you're going dressed in such a lovely horse riding getty-up," Freddy said.

"Yes. Thanks." Claudia unbuttoned her cherry-red blazer. "It's not as chilly as I expected."

"Lucky for you, the weatherman says this snowy cold front from Canada's gonna hold off till noon." Freddy ran his sleeve over a smudge on the brass awning support. "But on Monday it's supposed to be warm and dry for the Arbor Day Parade."

"I couldn't care less if I ever spend another minute in wintry weather again." Claudia made a sour face.

"This is my eighty-first spring," the doorman declared. "I was born and raised in Mississippi but I'm partial to the four seasons of the North."

"In Florida we had five seasons: spring, hurricane season, love bug season, the holidays, and almost winter. During almost winter I didn't wear sandals." Claudia peered down at her riding boots. She could see her reflection in the black polish.

"On these streets you might wanna keep your feet covered at all times." Freddy kicked a cigarette butt.

"Why's the sidewalk wet? Did it rain?" Claudia couldn't remember hearing a storm during the night. But then…

"We had us a sick visitor from the tavern around the corner. Nothing a few hot buckets of water couldn't wash."

"I don't know how that rooster tavern stays in business," Claudia said. "I can almost smell the ancient dust and mold from here."

"Cock of the Flock's got history. Legend has it the place was first opened by a pirate lady. Been serving wine and spirits ever since 1797." The doorman stepped off the curb to hail a lone passing taxi. A yellow-checkered cab slowed and stopped in front of the building. Freddy held the door for Claudia. "Enjoy your horsy ride, Miss Peña, but be careful. The park ain't always so safe as it looks."

Seamus lost his urge to vomit after two laps around the park lake. Although his stomach had calmed, his brain was full of warring 'whys'.

Why did he smell like a wet canine? Why did jogging cure a liquor-liver hangover? Why did he get sugar cravings? But most of all, why did the werewolf who chomped Seamus's heart not turn him to dust and thin air?

Seamus remembered the night he'd been turned. He'd been lying awake in bed, eyes fixed on the shadowy ceiling. He was in one of his "I'm not worthy" moods, brooding the fact that he'd almost lost a close match, had no idea who his parents were, no home to call his own, and at seventeen the prospect of adulthood and moving out of the boys' home was looming heavy on the horizon. Seamus recalled that his anxious energy needed an outlet. He channeled it, as usual, into an adrenaline rush.

Seamus grabbed his clothes and sneaked out of St. Guinefort's through the kitchen delivery door. He removed a bike from the sports equipment shed and peddled down the deserted avenue, past the old clock tower, to an unguarded construction site.

Seamus carried his mountain bike up twelve floors of unfinished steel steps to the highest level of scaffolding. Could he get up enough speed along the three-foot-wide girder to leap across the chasm to the building beyond? As Seamus began the momentum ride to his launch, his back tire slid off the edge of the girder. He tried to simultaneously catch his balance and jam on the breaks, but the girder was slick with dust and dew.

Seamus and the Trek were on their way over the edge when a massive force snatched the teen off his bike. He was engulfed and confined by a wall of hot fur. Seamus saw two icy blue eyes and a pair of fangs just before the flesh on his chest was torn. The pain was excruciating, but brief. A physical warmth and mental calm replaced hurt and terror just before Seamus's world went black.

The attacking beast left Seamus's turning body secured to the steel crossbeams where the teen had been attempting his stunt.

When Seamus awoke he was on his side. The first thing he noticed was his bike, down on the ground, twelve floors below him, unbroken. Seamus was positive it hadn't fallen. Seamus shifted focus to his chest. Although his T-shirt was ripped, the skin beneath it bore no blood or gash or scars. He breathed in a sigh of puzzled relief. Instead of weakness or pain, he felt strength and energy. Seamus tested this new found vigor by ripping free of the chords that bound him to the metal girder. The thick wires tore like tissue paper.

Seamus stood and stretched and mulled over his predicament. Maybe he was dead? Maybe he was dreaming? Maybe he'd been transformed into a superhero? Whatever the case, it was worth a curiosity test.

Seamus began running along the steel beam until he picked up enough speed and momentum to jump—clear across to the other side of the span and onto the roof of the next building. He landed with a THUD and tumbled hard through a pile of construction debris. Seamus lay without pain, battered and broken. He watched as his bones, scrapes, and abrasions healed before his bewildered eyes.

Seamus put his money on "superhero" until his first werewolf transformation. Afterwards, he considered placing a cryptic ad in the newspaper personals: *Leave anyone undead and hairy? He's looking for you and wants to know why.* Seamus imagined the responses; New City was full of kooks.

Every day as Seamus ran through Midtown Gardens he wondered about his eternal dilemma, and every night he fantasized about the gorgeous phantom girl who appeared at his kills, and who'd over the years developed into an even more beautiful phantom woman. Was she actually alive or was she a teen's fantasy that had blossomed big boobs and curvy hips?

Seamus answered himself. "Maybe I just REALLY need a girlfriend."

Early morning runners and bikers began crowding the lake's jogging path. Seamus heeded the Sarge's command and veered onto the deserted equestrian trail.

A lone female rider galloped along the path atop a blonde horse. The anxious palomino drew its ears back and began bucking, and rearing long before Seamus came into view. Its stunned rider was thrown from her mount, into a blooming azalea bush. The gelding retreated alone down the dusty path.

From fifty yards away, Seamus smelled the animal's fear and heard a female's distressed cry. He sprinted to her aid.

Seamus arrived in time to watch the fallen rider remove herself from the bush's tangled grasp. She took off her helmet, untied her long brunette hair, and wobbled over to a large rock where she sat. She gave herself a stunned moment before brushing leaves from her red blazer and checking her limbs. She felt someone staring. She looked up.

Seamus the jogger was ogling. He couldn't move, or believe his big green eyes.

"It's rude to gawk at an almost badly hurt person," the rider declared, taking off her black boot and removing a bit of twig. "Does your dog bite? Hope he didn't chase after Pirate." She put her boot back on. "Can't believe Pirate threw me."

Seamus wanted to shout, "It's you!"

"Have a cell phone?" she asked. "Mine is in the saddlebag. The groom will worry when my horse returns to the stable without me."

Seamus tried to reply, but no words formed, only thoughts. *Phantom woman.*

"Are you going to help me?" The rider's tone bordered on impatient.

Seamus uttered a noise that sounded a lot like a loud growl before finding his voice. "It's OK. Really, I'm a police officer." He unhooked a badge from his shorts and presented it. "There's no reason to be alarmed." Seamus hoped he'd sounded reassuring.

"You growled at me." The elegant rider seemed as surprised as she was concerned about officer's non-verbal communication.

The last thing Seamus needed was Sarge getting a call about a growling patrolman on the horse path. "Sorry if I scared you. I growl sometimes when I'm thrown off guard." *It's the phantom woman, or her waking twin.* Seamus was positive.

"You were thrown off guard? I'm the one who was abruptly tossed into a bush by my spooked horse."

"I don't growl very often," he lied. "Only when I haven't eaten in a while."

"So which was it? Surprise or hunger?" She folded her arms and smiled.

"Both. I just finished a night shift. I need some breakfast." Seamus patted his washboard stomach. "My workouts are usually uneventful. It's not everyday I run into an attractive woman upside down in the azaleas."

"At least you didn't howl at me. After last night, I'd have panicked it if you started howling and hopping around."

Seamus wanted to ask why.

"I should walk back to the barn." She straightened her riding jacket.

Seamus offered his hand. "Let me help you."

She took it. The moment their skin touched, the rider's knees turned to jelly. She wrapped her arms around Seamus to keep from falling.

"Are you OK?" Seamus's face was inches from his phantom woman. Resisting the urge to kiss her was difficult. Very difficult.

"I saw…" she stammered.

"What?" Seamus wanted to know.

"Nothing… I…I thought I saw something… when you touched me…"

"If you're still shaky from the fall. I could carry you back to the barn." Seamus hoped she'd take him up on his chivalrous offer.

"I'll be OK," she laughed. Her eyes met Seamus's gaze. "They're green."

"Green?" Seamus repeated, fearing he might have some rotten Mickey bits still stuck in his teeth.

"Your eyes. They're the same green as… Like two emeralds."

"Oh, yeah. I have green eyes." Seamus was relieved. "Ah, and your eyes are like two M&Ms, the dark brown ones. It's a metaphor."

"Actually, it's a simile," Phantom Woman corrected.

"Brains and beauty." Seamus wasn't sure he cared about brains, although there was something really annoying about talking to an idiot. As a cop, he encountered lots of them. Mickey for example. However, at the moment Seamus was glad Mickey's soused liver had led him to Claudia.

The rider released her support hug. She took two steps unassisted. "Nothing's broken. I can walk. See?"

"Can't stop staring." Seamus held out his arm. "How about a police escort back to the barn?"

Phantom Woman obliged. "Sure. Where's your dog? I smell him, but I don't see him. Here doggy!" She canvassed the woods. "You call him."

Seamus didn't reply.

Claudia sniffed Seamus's t-shirt. "I just realized where it's coming from!"

"You're gonna tell me I stink like a dog," Seamus said in a-matter-of-fact-tone.

"You do! A wet dog!" the rider squealed. "That's so weird!"

Seamus was used to ribbing, but her laughter stung. "Ouch."

"I didn't mean you're weird. I meant the dog smell. That's one strong stench!"

"You seem to say whatever comes to mind," Seamus remarked.

"So I've been told," she replied with a chuckle.

"If you're wondering, I shower often, *and* use soap," Seamus countered.

"Did you ever think about shaving your body and wearing cologne?"

"Why? You prefer poodles?"

Claudia laughed. "Dog odor's not so bad. I guess I could get used to dog."

"Glad to hear it." He was.

"Should I call you police dog?" she asked.

"Sorry. My name is Seamus, Seamus Sullivan."

"Nice to meet you," the rider replied. "I'm Claudia."

"Claudia," Seamus repeated. He liked the sound of her name. Strong, yet feminine. "I run this path every morning and this is the first time I've had the pleasure of knocking you off your horse."

"Pirate is usually bombproof." Claudia rubbed her forearm and adjusted her neck. "Something must have really scared him, but I'm sure it wasn't you."

Seamus knew better. "Do you ride often?"

"Most days, but not this early. I couldn't sleep last night." She looked away.

"Insomnia?" Seamus was fishing for information.

"Nightmares."

"What kind of nightmares?" Seamus wondered aloud.

"Familiar ones. But my first interrupted sleep since moving here from Florida, so I'm not complaining."

"Well then, welcome to New City, home of occasional sleepless nights and spooky horse trails."

"And the Bronx Bombers," Claudia added.

"Baseball fan?"

"You could say that," she replied.

"I used to be a Bombers fanatic when I was a kid, until Sternfenner bought the team and all the over-priced prima-donnas he could get his grubby rich fingers on. This year is the worst."

He didn't catch Claudia's growing glare.

"Alejandro Peña isn't worth a half billion dollars. The guy's a slap in the face to every dad who can't afford to buy himself and his kid a ballpark seat in pigeon heaven. Forget a box seat behind home plate or the dugout, gotta mortgage the farm for that rich-guy privilege."

"Television and advertising revenue pays player salaries, not admission and pretzel prices," Claudia bristled.

"Corporate greed, any way you slice it," Seamus remarked.

"It may be expensive to go to the ballpark these days," Claudia's voice rose an octave. "But don't blame ticket price inflation on Alejandro Peña."

"Why would Peña care if a former fan blamed him for salary gluttony?" Seamus asked unruffled. "As long as the guy collects his big fat paycheck."

"Oh yeah? It isn't just about the paycheck. Alejandro Peña loves the game and he happens to be a kind, caring man who also gives back to the community. I know for a fact his youth foundation has provided educational grants and scholarships to hundreds of underprivileged children."

"Right. When did his PR people think that up?" Seamus mocked.

"The charity trust was established years ago, long before his Bombers contract."

"Whoopee! Give the guy a float in the Arbor Day parade." Seamus twirled his index finger. "Or maybe his head's so inflated he should be a character balloon?"

Claudia stopped walking. "For your information, police dog, Mayor Fink will honor The Alejandro Peña Foundation at a charity dinner next week." She put her hand on her hip. "Have you ever been honored by Mayor Fink? "

"Hey, I didn't know you had a crush on the guy or something. And *yes*, I have 'been honored' by Mayor Fink *and* his dog. They presented all five of my citations for valor and courage in the line of duty." Seamus blushed. He'd never before talked about his police medals with anyone but the Sarge. Seamus kept them in his sock drawer, with his spare bullets and pocket change.

"Wow, five citations; you're one courageous police dog. I'm impressed. But let's not change the subject," Claudia continued her defense. "I do not have a crush on Alejandro Peña. I respect him. He's a role model, a terrific guy."

"Who hangs out in strip clubs. Wonder if Mr. Role Model tips well?" Seamus could see he was getting Claudia's goat, and he was having fun with it.

Claudia countered again, this time with vexation. "So, what'd you win your five medals for? Being an undercover snoop doggy-dog? Does the city pay you to patrol titty bars and snitch on people? Is it a crime to look at boobs?" She got up in his face. "Or have purple hair?"

"I'm a boob fan, too." Seamus struggled not to focus on Claudia's chest. "We're losing our 'gazing into each other's eyes' good start here."

"Because you are a spy," she accused.

"I wasn't spying on the guy, but some paparazzi was. I saw his picture in the morning paper. Peña was walking out of a strip club. And FYI, I don't get the purple hair reference." Phantom woman's bare breasts appeared before his mind's eye. Seamus adjusted his running shorts.

Claudia turned away and began briskly walking towards the barn.

"Hey, wait up! You walk pretty fast for an almost badly hurt person."

Claudia increased her pace.

"OK, sorry, I shouldn't be critical of Alejandro Peña," Seamus said. I don't know the guy. Only know what I read in the newspapers, and the papers aren't always the best source of truthful information. Don't be mad. I'm sorry if I offended you."

"There's something about you…" Claudia's raised her eyebrows but didn't slow her stride. "Who are you, Seamus Sullivan?"

"Me?" *What does she know?* Seamus jogged along side her. "Bet you could beat your horse in a race."

"I get this feeling… you're sad, angry, scared, brave, wild, and reckless, all at the same time."

She can read me. "Oh, boy. It's that obvious?"

"What's the real reason you don't like Alejandro Peña?" she asked.

"Maybe I'm jealous." Seamus shrugged.

"Jealous of what?" Claudia probed without breaking stride.

"The fame. The money. Maybe I wish I were a great athlete, a boxer, maybe. Instead of a cop stuck on park patrol until he retires."

"If you have the talent," Claudia challenged. "What's stopping you?"

Seamus didn't answer. His canine ears could hear the commotion of nervous horses. They were getting close to the barn. The last thing Seamus needed was a werewolf-induced stampede. He stopped jogging and took hold of Claudia's arm. "Wait a minute."

Claudia paused.

"Look, I hope you're not gonna hold a grudge for what I said about the Bombers and Alejandro Peña."

"Doesn't sound like an apology."

"You're right." Seamus bent down on one knee and took Claudia's hand. "I am sorry for anything I said or did that may have offended you in any way, shape or form; it was never my intention."

Claudia smiled. "Apology accepted. You may rise."

Seamus hopped to his feet. "Can I make it up to you? How about breakfast?"

"Breakfast?" Claudia beamed. "You're asking me out?"

"I'm asking you out," Seamus said, trying to contain his eagerness. "The stable is close to here. You'll be safe finishing your return alone. I'll run back to the station house and shower, and see if I can find some cologne."

"I'd like very much to go on a date with you, Seamus Sullivan, even if you don't find some cologne."

"Really? Great. Ah, I know a little inn about an hour from here, over-looking the river. They serve the best frosted waffles with orange syrup."

"Sounds sweet."

"Don't go home and change or anything." He suppressed a howl. "I'll be right back. Will you stay and wait for me?" In his enthusiasm, Seamus began bounding, like a big happy puppy.

"I'll wait," Claudia promised.

"Perfect. Pick you up in half an hour, in the main parking lot, over by the WWI statue, the one —"

"I know where it is," Claudia chuckled. "Down, boy."

"Hope you don't mind motorcycles. Probably not if you ride horses. Anyway, you can wear my helmet."

"A motorcycle? In New City? And you'll be riding without a helmet? Seamus, you must have a death wish," Claudia remarked. "Or a very hard head."

Seamus couldn't wait to have Claudia behind him on the Beemer, her arms wrapped around his waist, her breasts pressed against …

His lusty thought was interrupted.

"Miss Peña! Miss Peña! A frenzied stableman came sprinting down the riding path towards Claudia and Seamus. "Miss Peña, I was so worried! Pirate returned to the barn without you! I didn't have your home number. I would have called your brother. Thank goodness you're not hurt!"

"Miss Peña?" Seamus repeated, most intrigued. A sly smile slid across his lips, "Any relation to Alejandro Peña?"

"You promised me breakfast, Officer Sullivan," Claudia replied in a playful haughty tone. "We'll continue our baseball chat later. Now run along and get your shower." Claudia flashed him a devious grin.

The sun peeked through the tree canopy and illuminated Claudia's chocolate hair, honey skin, and perfect curves.

It has to be her. Seamus couldn't resist. "Of course, Miss Peña. But, I have a request. After the baseball chat, may we discuss last night?"

"Last night?" Claudia asked, looking puzzled.

Seamus's green eyes glowed. "Last night, you visited me, wearing those pretty pink paisley pajamas."

"*¡Díos mío!*" she gasped.

"I thought so."

Chapter 6

GODS' HOUNDS

Father X. Francis Benedict retired alone to his private study following Saturday morning devotions. The room was grand and elegant, in an ancient stale sort of way. The library was decorated with European antiques. A well-stocked Victorian sideboard, a claw-foot desk, and two matching velvet armchairs positioned across from a leather fireside sofa comprised the furnishings. Carved oak bookshelves laden with leather-bound volumes lined the twelve-foot walls.

Father Benedict secured the study doors and drew a pair of brocade drapes before removing his wire-rimmed spectacles. He unfastened the white starched collar and sash of his priest garb. The black robe contrasted with his flaxen hair. The padre stretched and shifted his body in the dimness, like a nocturnal animal awakening from slumber. His countenance transformed from a character in his December years, to the actor who embodied a natural full summer bloom.

Father Benedict reached with ease for a well-worn volume high on the library bookshelf: FAMOUS WITCH AND WEREWOLF TRIALS. A tasseled marker indicated the chapter he sought.

The first-ever documented lycanthrope trial was held in 1792, in Livonia, an area east of the Baltic Sea. The werewolf case implicated a foreigner known only as Sevlow.

According to surviving court transcripts, a beggar woman beaten and robbed by thieves and left for dying, had witnessed Sevlow transform from man into wolf beast. He pursued her assailants. After recovering from her injuries, the woman notified authorities, who arrested Sevlow, in his human form.

Sevlow was not charged for the murder of the thieves, since no corpses or living persons associated with the alleged crime were ever found. However, Sevlow was brought up on more serious charges.

At Sevlow's trial, many of the judges were skeptical of the woman's account. In spite of this, Sevlow confessed to being a werewolf, saying his earthly mission was godly and that he, along with a band of other commissioned werewolves, fought against the demons of hell on earth.

The judges were astounded by such implausible testimony.

Sevlow insisted werewolves were hounds of gods who assisted mankind by preventing Beelzebub and his minions from inflicting murderous mayhem.

If it were not for werewolves culling evil from the flock, proclaimed Sevlow, all mankind would suffer and eventually succumb to the forces of darkness.

When probed about the origin of werewolves, Sevlow explained that the formation of werewolves came about in one of two ways.

One, werewolves were created in Heaven by the gods and sent directly to earth where they embarked upon their given missions.

Two, werewolves could be crafted from humans when immediate need for support arose. Although human reinforcements were a rarity, Sevlow lamented, for only virtuous souls were chosen to become a hound of the gods.

According to Sevlow, new hounds instinctively preyed upon corrupted souls during the full moon phase, but they could also transform and execute at any time, if provoked by evil.

Sevlow reported that he was in his third century of the gods' service, but he knew other werewolves who had been deployed for much longer.

Despite the judges' requests, Sevlow refused to elaborate on the werewolves' return to Heaven.

The dubious judges pressed for a retraction, but Sevlow was determined in his admission.

Sevlow also refused to confess his sins to a parish priest who was sent to rebuke him for polytheism and blasphemy. Sevlow insisted that he was a better man than any priest, and to his knowledge, no priest had ever proven righteous enough to be recruited by the gods or the werewolves.

The courtroom erupted in laughter.

After much deliberation, the presiding judge sentenced Sevlow to ten lashes for acts of idolatry, lycanthropy, and superstitious beliefs. He was further condemned to be set adrift on a skiff without water or provisions, and with strict instructions to never again return to Livonia, should he survive.

The lashes were, however, not given. No man could be found who would take a whip to the werewolf.

Father X. Francis Benedict reinserted the chapter marker and returned the book to its place on the shelf and then spoke an unwritten postscript.

"Sevlow survived the tempest without incident. The werewolf was salvaged a fortnight later by buccaneers." The clergyman's thin lips curved into a faint grin. "No worse for wear. In 1797, Sevlow arrived in New City with the gods' orders and abundant riches." Father Benedict placed a gentle hand upon a large plumed chapeau that adorned his study wall. "Sevlow wasn't alone," he whispered.

Chapter 7

PUPPY LOVE

The Riverview Café, located in the former boathouse of the Riverview Inn, was deserted except for Seamus and Claudia.

The lone off-season cook/waitress prepared and served breakfast before dashing back to the inn parlor to watch morning game shows. But not before leaving her sole patrons the check, extra napkins, and a large scented candle.

Seamus didn't drive an hour for the service. He was anxious to be in an out-of-the-way locale with his phantom woman. They were all alone; he was staring. If he'd been wearing his tail, it would be wagging.

"A werewolf? My dreams would make sense if that were true, but at the same time your claim is hard to believe." Claudia added a liberal splash of three-alarm sauce to her cheesy salsa omelet. "Are you sure you're not just trying to impress me with your wild wolf stories?"

"If Ms. Congeniality ever returns I can order you a fire extinguisher to go with your eggs."

"Ha-ha. I like my food spicy, and my guys sweet. Anyway, I didn't criticize you for putting sugar *and* syrup on frosted orange waffles. Pity the dentist who has to fill your cavities. If you really are a werewolf."

"I don't get cavities and I really am a werewolf. And on the contrary, I like my women spicy and my food sweet." Seamus teased in his best Rico Suave voice, "You are the spiciest woman I have ever met. You are Tabasco— red, hot, picante, zesty."

"Did you read that off the back of the bottle?" Claudia asked with a smile. "Or do you make things up as you go along?"

"There are pick-up lines on the back of the Tabasco bottle?" Seamus examined the label. "Do not consume while operating heavy machinery. Keep away from open flames. Once used rectally, the bottle should not be used orally."

Claudia grabbed the little bottle and examined it. "It does not say that!"

Seamus scratched his back with a spoon. "Wonder how come I don't often get dates with beautiful, rich, pampered, debutantes?"

"I come from hard-working Cuban immigrant stock."

"Really?"

"Really. My parents owned Casa Havana, a small family-style restaurant in Hollywood, Florida."

"Prosperous restaurateurs."

"Hardly. The most frivolous thing they ever splurged on was a used speedboat, after my brother received his baseball scholarship from the Miami University Thunderstorms." She looked away. "I wish they hadn't."

Seamus detected a change in Claudia's tone. "You OK?"

She appeared to be forcing a smile. "Fine, I remembered something sad."

"Someone wear the same dress as you to the coming out ball?"

Claudia laughed. "I'm not a debutante." She stirred her tea.

Seamus leaned back in his chair. "But you don't deny being the gorgeous and pampered sister of baseball's richest player?"

Claudia responded with mischief in her voice, "I am what I am."

"You have no idea how wild you have made me these past few years."

"What? Before our colliding dreams you were a wallflower?"

"Hmmm…I wouldn't say that." Seamus plopped a glob of jam into his OJ.

"Besides being the anti-diabetic, tell me about yourself, Seamus Sullivan. Where'd you grow up? Do you have siblings? Where do your parents live?"

"I already told you the most important thing about me, besides, I hate interviews."

"This is not an interview. It's a discussion. We're getting to know one another."

"Too many questions."

"Questions are a necessary component of conversation."

"Alright. Horses have four legs. True or false?"

"What?"

"Is that your final answer?"

"True. My final answer is true; horses have four legs."

"Bzzz, wrong. Horses have three legs. The fourth leg is actually an extension of the tail bone."

"No, it's not!"

"Ducks like water. True or false?"

Claudia was wise to his silly game. "False."

"Bing, bing! Correct! Ducks only spend most of their time in water because they dislike land more. Question three..."

"No more questions!" she pleaded.

"Sure, have it your way. Q & A has been suspended until further notice."

Claudia sighed and folded her arms, making her cleavage more pronounced.

"Arrgh!" Seamus choked on his waffle. "You did that on purpose."

"What?" Claudia bit a corner of toast and licked a trace of butter from her lip.

"That, and the way you speak, move, breathe. You don't have an unfeminine bone in your body. Bet you hated PE."

"Not true." Claudia replied. "I used to be a ball girl."

"Used to? What happened?"

"Polyester started clinging to my curves." Claudia shrugged. "Guys on Alex's team noticed."

"I'm sure they did."

"My brother bribed me out of the dugout."

"Ultimately your decision to accept the carrot, or not."

"The uniform was itchy and the cap squished my hair," Claudia said. "That's when Alex bought me Pirate."

"A horse. A small price to pay for sanity. I would have punched half the guys on the team just for looking at my sister, if I had one."

"Teammates or sister?"

"Both."

"You can't pummel people for looking."

"Why not?"

"C'mon." Claudia rolled her eyes. "You're a police officer. Duh!"

"Not a monster?" Seamus said.

"Despite being a bit of a wise guy, you've opened doors for me, pulled out my chair, behaved like an absolute gentleman." Claudia shook her head. "You don't want my impression of you to slip, Officer Sullivan."

Seamus sat up straight. "Oh, no, not ebb tide. Gimme a chance to recover here. My mind's still foggy. All that pressing and grabbing you did on the ride up. I had to brain-sing cartoon theme songs to keep from crashing. Who lives in a pineapple under the sea… *Stay-on-the-road…* Absorbent and yellow and porous is he… *I've-seen-her-nude…*"

"Seamus!" Claudia cried.

"It's true. And it's all I could think about while you *squeezed* me while I tried to keep my bike glued to the road, like a safe driver, and a gentleman."

"That spooning and gripping on the trip up was motivated by fear, not desire."

Seamus was staring again. "You must drive the guys at school nuts, too."

"I quit school when I was 10."

"Grammar school drop-out? I won't ask you to figure the tip."

"I'm very good in math. I've been home schooled."

"Alex has many talents."

"My brother hired tutors and governesses. Like Mrs. Doubtfire."

"Cross-dressers?"

"Big-boned British women," Claudia chuckled.

"I'm glad I make you laugh." Seamus examined the bill. He took two twenties from his billfold. "No hurry. This table-with-a-view is ours until tourist season, or until you get sick of me gawking. Whichever comes first."

"Any pictures in your wallet?" Claudia reached across the table.

"How'd I know you'd ask that?" Seamus handed it over. "Just the mug shots on my driver's license and police ID."

Claudia studied the license in silence.

"There won't be a test," Seamus said before eating a spoonful of sugar.

"A birthday coming up, April 17th; you're almost 22."

"Sorta." Seamus wasn't up for explaining his perpetual age dilemma. He'd met with enough skepticism following his 'I'm a werewolf' confession.

"You're an Aries." Claudia returned his wallet. "Tell a fiery Aries man he can't do something, and you've just given him a mission."

Seamus slipped the wallet back into his pocket. "That so? I've been on a mission to uncover the mystery of my phantom woman."

"Your phantom woman? That's what you called me?" Claudia took a sip of tea.

Seamus was quiet for a spell. He thought back to the first time he'd seen her. His second kill. His mood mellowed. "I didn't expect she'd be real."

"You thought I was a ghost?"

"I don't believe in ghosts." Seamus downed the last of his jelly-filled OJ.

"But you believe in werewolves?" Claudia said, with more than a smattering of cynicism in her tone.

"Yep. And I'm not the only lupus in town."

"Then where are the others?"

"Out there…Somewhere." As if on queue, Seamus heard howling in the distance. He glanced out the window at his motorcycle. It was the only vehicle in the parking lot. Seamus checked the table. His bike key was still beside the saltshaker.

"Have you searched? Made inquires?"

"Nope." Seamus refocused his attention once again on his date.

"How come?" Claudia asked. "I'd be curious enough to use my werewolf powers to hunt him down."

"The werewolf found me once. I believe he'll find me again," Seamus said. "When the time is right, he'll come out of hiding."

"You really think you're being watched? By the one who attacked you?" A tinge of trepidation resonated in Claudia's voice.

"For sure." Seamus nodded. "I know he's out there, keeping tabs on me."

Claudia eased her chair closer.

Their knees touched.

Claudia swallowed. She reached across the table and grasped Seamus's hand.

Seamus could feel the spirit of his mortal heart racing inside his chest. It sent butterflies fluttering to his stomach, and electricity rushing through his veins. "Phantom woman is somehow connected to who I've become." Seamus spoke his thought.

Claudia nodded, but remained silent.

"There's a bond between us." He paused for her reply. "You know something."

Claudia looked away. "You think I have answers."

"Don't leave me in the dark," Seamus pleaded. "Why have you been coming to my kills, watching me?"

"I don't know... My visions..." Claudia's voice trailed.

"What? Tell me." Seamus's curiosity was ablaze.

"They have something to do with..." she hesitated.

Their eyes met and fixed.

Seamus was deluged by wave of passion. He'd fallen for phantom woman long ago, hook, line and sinker. He started to speak, and then stopped himself.

"What?" Claudia asked. "Are you keeping another secret?"

"Sometimes I'd plan a kill, so you'd visit me," Seamus confessed. "I haven't told this to anyone." Seamus shook his head. "Sarge would never forgive me if he knew."

"Knew what?" Claudia looked puzzled, and a little frightened.

"I'd try to force a change whenever I got the urge to see you."

"You can *will* yourself to be a werewolf?" Claudia asked.

"Not exactly, but New City has a dark side," Seamus said. "Let's just say the bad guys aren't hard to find."

"You mean you'd pick a fight?"

"More like I'd put myself in the wrong place at the right time."

"The werewolf as sacrificial lamb," Claudia said. "Let someone attack you?"

"More like a vigilante in disguise," Seamus answered in a matter-of-fact tone. "Predators want victims. Better me than a little old lady, or some kid riding his bike home from school. There are sick creeps and perverts everywhere."

Claudia let go of Seamus's hand. "You know what I think?"

"Huh?"

"I think we simultaneously dream about werewolf monsters, and then somehow our nightmares mingle, crossed radio signals. The events we witness are an impression, a longing, not a reality," Claudia spoke with confidence. "Maybe we want to 'transform' ourselves into someone different. Someone who isn't a loner, someone who's part of a group, a pack, like a wolf."

69

"Sounds feasible, Sigmund Freud, but way off base. Maybe you wake up, but I live my nightmares, every day and night. I'm undead," Seamus said.

"You're flesh and blood and mortal soul," Claudia replied. "Same as I am."

"I killed Mickey Stella last night, after he murdered me," Seamus reminded. "I died, then got up and took revenge."

"Don't say that, Seamus." Claudia turned away, a look of disgust etched across her pretty face.

"You saw me kill. I decapitated the guy and disemboweled his blubbery corpse."

Claudia paled. She pressed her napkin to her lips.

"These aren't just bad dreams. They're a worse reality. I kill people, Claudia. Can't deny what you've seen." His voice was cold.

"I'm not in denial," Claudia retorted. "Maybe it's *you* who can't grasp the truth. What proof do you have? Disgusting images, missing persons, and our wolf dreams could very well be a grotesque, imaginary world we both enter into while we're in sleep mode."

"Claudia, I have proof that I went to work last night. Not to sleep, like you," said Seamus. "Mickey's mama is searching for her dead son and the Sarge is not happy about it. I'm in the *real* doghouse at the moment because I'm a *real* werewolf."

"No," she insisted. "I don't believe you're a werewolf."

"Oh, yeah?" Seamus lunged forward and seized Claudia's fork. He jammed the steely prongs into his cheek. Warm blood spurted onto his face, Claudia's white blouse, the checkered tablecloth.

Claudia shrieked in horror.

Seamus pushed the fork deeper into his skin and gouged out a hunk of flesh and flung it onto her plate.

"Stop! You're crazy!" Claudia bolted from her chair and ran for the door.

Seamus caught hold of her hair. Claudia's head jerked.

"Ow!" she screamed. "Get away!"

"In a minute you'll see what I am." His voice was calm and unthreatening.

"Let me go!" Claudia cried and fell to her knees. "Please, don't hurt me."

Seamus caged her in his rock-hard arms.

She tried to wiggle free. It was no use. Seamus had the strength of ten men.

Seamus held Claudia and pressed his bloody face against her sweet-smelling hair. "Don't move." He waited.

Claudia remained still and sobbed.

It was time. "Now, Claudia. Look at me," Seamus instructed.

"No. Please, let me go," she replied through a river of tears.

Seamus released his grip and turned her face towards his.

Claudia closed her eyes. "Don't hurt me!"

"I haven't hurt you. I won't hurt you."

"Go away!" she cried. "I'm afraid!"

"It's OK." He wrapped his arms around her once again.

"No."

"Claudia, open your eyes… please."

"You gouged your own face," Claudia gagged. "You're sick!"

"Please… Shhh…" Seamus whispered. "Trust me."

Claudia opened her downcast eyes. "My bloody blouse?"

"It's clean. Now, please, look at me."

"Seamus… your cheek…" Claudia touched him.

He guided her hand. "I'm healed. No blood. No scar."

"But…" Claudia wept. "Why? How did you do that?"

Seamus wiped her tears. "I had to make you see that I was telling the truth. I'm a werewolf. I'm undead."

"I thought you were going to kill me." Her tears continued to flow.

"I'd never harm you." Seamus stroked her hair. "I'm sorry you were scared." Seamus lifted her chin. Claudia was shivering and breathless as he laced his arms beneath her shoulders and hair. The brilliance in his eyes was pure feral emotion. "I'm going to kiss you," he whispered, nuzzling her cheek, pawing her as she hugged him back; her body still quivering.

Seamus pressed his mouth to hers.

She didn't resist.

He tasted her salty tears, her warm soft tongue.

Claudia's body relaxed.

Seamus detected an in and made a stealthy try for second base.

Claudia blocked with a forearm sweep.

Seamus smiled, like an unconstrained child pondering his next move. He gazed down at her. "You have no idea—"

Claudia's return kiss silenced him.

Seamus wanted to consume her, devour her. He kissed harder and sneaked his southpaw beneath her untucked blouse. Claudia's skin was warm and smooth. He envisioned himself sliding into home plate. Seamus pressed himself against her as his palm swept along the small of her back. His fingers making a play for her bra hook.

Claudia balked. "Wait!"

Seamus's hand retreated. He gave Claudia a sheepish look, like a hound dog just scolded for messing where he shouldn't have.

"It's OK," Claudia mumbled, adjusting her skewed blouse. "Things are just sort of surreal; it's all happening too fast. Not to mention we're in a restaurant."

"I got carried away," Seamus apologized.

"Me too." Claudia sighed. "Yeah. It's been a bizarre morning." She brushed her hair away from her flushed cheek.

"Don't forget last night," Seamus added.

"I would if I could. This has been one of the weirdest 24 hours of my life."

"Not 'the' weirdest?" Seamus said. "I can't wait to get to know you better."

"You will… for sure." Claudia smiled. "Despite *that* outburst, I like you, Seamus the werewolf." She shook her head. "Wow, that sounds crazy. Let's just take it a little slower... even if you have seen me naked."

He groaned.

"What's the matter?"

Seamus didn't dare explain his physical reaction to their kiss. "I have to hit the men's room."

"You in pain?" Claudia's expression conveyed her concern. "Maybe you shouldn't have stuck that fork into your face."

"I've done worse."

Claudia raised an eyebrow.

"When I return from the men's room, want to take a walk down by the river?"

"Sure. I wouldn't mind getting out of here. I need some fresh air."

Seamus trotted to the loo and stood before the urinal waiting for excitement to subside. He forced himself to envision disagreeable images. *Kill vomit, weevils in the cereal box… Sarge's yellow fingernail clippings.* Seamus peed, washed his hands, then ran his damp fingers through his wavy black hair, and grinned into the mirror. Seamus couldn't remember a better day, ever. He hurried back to his date.

The dining room was deserted.

Claudia's red handbag hung on the post of her chair. Seamus didn't have a whole lot of experience with females, but he knew for a fact they didn't go to the bathroom without their purses.

His motorcycle key wasn't next to the salt shaker. Seamus grabbed Claudia's pocketbook and sprinted out the door.

The Beemer was gone. Seamus reclaimed his discarded bike helmet from the parking lot gravel. His emerald eyes began to glow. "Don't go getting all hairy," he said aloud to himself. "Claudia, I have to find Claudia." His pupils dilated. "Stop turning! Raindrops on roses, whiskers on kittens, bright copper kettles, and Claudia wearing that black Brazilian thong."

The anger left his body.

Seamus's police-sense kicked in. He canvassed the area. There, in plain sight, was a matchbook. He picked it up. "Cock of the Flock," Seamus read before lifting the cover. There was something written on the inside flap: *Tag! You're it!*

Chapter 8

HIDE AND SEEK

Claudia awoke in a dank shadowy stone space. The room was dim, long, and narrow, lit by a lone-lighted torch that hung on the wall. Her head pounded. There was a fog in her brain and her body felt constricted. She was lying on a wooden cot beneath a heavy brocaded quilt. Claudia wiggled free. She pushed the covers off and swung her feet onto the cold cobbled floor. She wasn't wearing her riding boots. *It smells like a museum.* To her shock, she spotted a man dressed in a black floor-length robe with a white stiff collar and rope sash seated in the dark corner of the room. Claudia stopped mid-breath and held still. It was odd. The man appeared to be reading a book without benefit of light. Even in the shadowiness Claudia could see his hair, pale blonde, one hue shy of white. She stared at his long, slim fingers and remembered the café, and the abrasive medicinal smell that preceded her unconsciousness. Claudia never had the chance to scream. Claudia's anger overtook her fear. "Where am I?" she demanded.

The robed man placed a marker inside the book and peered above his reading glasses. He lit a candle, but didn't reply to her question.

Claudia studied the man's face. He appeared to be about Alex's age. His features were distinct and attractive, but at the same time peculiar and out-of-date. It was as if her captor had somehow stepped out of a Byzantine mosaic and into the 21st century. "Who are you?" Her tone was more timid than before.

The robed man spoke without hurry. "There are more things in Heaven and Earth, Horatio, than are dreamt of in your philosophy."

He had a foreign accent. Claudia couldn't place it.

The man set his book down. His eyes remained fixed and expressionless. "Do you enjoy Shakespeare, Miss Peña?"

Claudia's heart leapt. "How do you know my name?

"Before I answer your question, please be assured I mean you no harm." His voice was smooth and cordial.

It was the second time in one day Claudia had been promised her safety following a terrifying event. This time she wasn't buying it. "What do you consider drugging and kidnapping?" she retorted. "You've *already* harmed me."

Her captor stood. He removed the torch and used it to light a trail of lanterns along the corridor. The room was soon bathed in a bright amber glow.

Claudia watched his every move with keen interest. *Where's the nearest door?* She wanted to run, scream, and call her brother. She wished her parents would appear and explain what was happening. *Mami, Papi where are you?*

They did not appear.

The robed man returned the torch to its holder and sat back down across from Claudia. "Perhaps in brighter light I will appear less ominous." He smiled, folding his hands on his lap.

Claudia refused to allow herself to be swayed by the robed man's amiable expression, his striking aquamarine eyes, his pious attire, or the fact that her supernatural radar detected a serene goodness about him.

She collected herself before questioning him again. "How do I know that I'm safe? That you're a trustworthy priest?"

Her captor made a throaty hum of amusement, as if responding to a private joke. "I have taken no vows to any church or religion."

"Then whom do you work for?"

"I am a high-ranking envoy of the gods, Miss Peña."

"A bishop?"

Her host threw back his head and laughed. "If I may be so bold, where I come from, werewolf trumps Pope."

"Werewolf!" Claudia shrieked.

"A hound of the gods." He bowed with reverence.

"You, you are the one who turned Seamus into a werewolf!"

"Yes. Seamus is indeed a werewolf of my making." The creator spoke with pride.

"You attacked Seamus and left him for dead." The hairs on Claudia's arms prickled. She felt a lump forming in her throat.

"I left him *undead*," the werewolf corrected.

"Why? What did he ever do to you?" Claudia became protective.

"It is what Seamus almost did to himself that altered my schedule." The werewolf appeared to consider whether or not to elaborate. He did not.

"Because Seamus messed up your schedule, you took his life?"

"Seamus has been given a gift, Ms. Peña."

Claudia rolled her eyes. "Yeah, right."

"I don't expect you to comprehend this situation or my motives."

"Try me," she huffed. "What I know might shock you. I'm not your average teenager."

"No, you are not," the werewolf replied through a faint grin. "It is unfortunate, but I do not have time to discuss this matter in more detail."

"Just tell me *why* you picked Seamus." Claudia wanted to know if her instincts about Seamus were correct. *Is he a good guy?*

"Reinforcements." The werewolf hesitated for a moment, and then continued. "I will tell you that when I turned Seamus he was young and headstrong, the combination made him what you might call a daredevil, but his heart is virtuous and his spirit brave and resilient." The werewolf beamed like a father speaking about his son. "I have monitored Seamus's police work these past few years."

"Spying," Claudia said. She recalled her manners. "Watching out for him."

The werewolf smiled. "There is an important mission pending and it is time for your boyfriend to join the pack."

"He's not my boyfriend." Claudia blushed. "We met for the first time today."

"I misspoke." The werewolf bowed. "I assumed from your breakfast that…" He paused. "That you two were more than new acquaintances."

"Well, sort of." Claudia decided not to elaborate. "What do I have to do with any of this, this pack and pending mission?"

The werewolf didn't answer.

Claudia found his purposeful silences somewhat annoying.

The padre left his seat and wandered over to a protruding section of the stone wall. He ran his fingers along a series of metal plates that had turned green with age.

"Where are we?" Claudia leaned forward and squinted. She was able to decipher the writing. There were names on the plates followed by a series of dates. The plates were grave markers. "This is a tomb!" Claudia cried.

The werewolf returned to his chair and faced her. He seemed to be pondering his next words.

Claudia's heart pounded; dread churned her stomach. She had an urge to vomit.

"I must keep you hidden for now, in a place where Seamus will not find you."

"I haven't done anything to you or to Seamus." She tried hard not to cry. "Why do I have to stay hidden away in a tomb?"

"Seamus has been left alone these past few years, but today he will be introduced to his pack for the first time, and he will be asked to fight along side them. Presently, Seamus has no allegiance to the pack. However, based on restaurant observations, I believe

Seamus would fight to keep you safe, and he would fight to see you again, sooner rather than later."

"Later? Later than what?" Claudia's mind was racing. "How long do you plan to keep me a pawn in this place?"

The werewolf shook his head. "That will depend on a number of factors."

Claudia heard a faint rustle and whispering.

The werewolf gave no indication that he heard it too.

Maybe they weren't alone. Claudia wondered if the white-haired werewolf knew she was Seamus's phantom woman, or if he had one of his own.

"I did not anticipate that Seamus would fall in love, so soon," the werewolf said.

Claudia turned away, feeling both embarrassed *and* thrilled.

"I have known Seamus for many years. Up until now he has been quite the loner," the werewolf said in earnest. "However, as you may have already gleaned from life, Miss Peña, there is no such thing as a coincidence. You and Seamus have come together for a reason. One of which is purpose. Your stay here will give my daring recruit a reason to remain focused on his duties."

Claudia envisioned ferocious werewolves battling on the streets of New City. It didn't make sense. Like a bad B movie. "Is Seamus in danger?"

"If he loses concentration." The werewolf's voice trailed. "His safety could be compromised."

Claudia felt a chill run up her spine. Too many odd things were happening too fast. She had to find a way to escape, to warn Seamus.

"I give my word. I will keep you safe, as long as you remain hidden."

"On a stale cot in a musty tomb? How long do I have to stay in this medieval Motel 6?" Claudia folded her arms.

The werewolf smiled, displaying perfect white teeth. "This afternoon I will bring you a supply of food and drink and books to read. Our school library is very well stocked."

"School library?"

Her captor nodded. "I hope this confinement will not prompt you to rescind your generous scholarship offer, Miss Peña. The boys at St. Guinefort's are deserving of your brother's charitable gift. It is not their fault a werewolf governs the home, and has for more decades than a rosary." He touched the knotted string of wooden beads that hung from the sash around his waist.

Claudia's jaw dropped. "You're Father Benedict!"

"Not exactly," the werewolf explained. "There *was* a Father X. Francis Benedict, many years ago. I was with him when he died."

"You killed Fr. Benedict?" She recoiled.

"I did not, Miss Peña. Please, rest assured." The werewolf's voice was calm and courteous. "Father Benedict was a fine and frequent customer."

"Customer?" Claudia was now completely confused.

"I have owned the Cock of the Flock since 1797," the werewolf said.

"But—" Claudia attempted to interrupt.

The werewolf seemed to anticipate her next question. "It is not the time to explain how a werewolf came to be proprietor of a tavern, and has remained so for over two hundred years." The werewolf continued his story. "Father Benedict visited most evenings for a nightcap. The padre was a loquacious man, with a preference for whiskey."

A blabbermouth drunk, thought Claudia. She'd seen the characters that hung out at the dusty rooster dive.

"One evening Father Benedict came in, looking gloomy and pallid and complaining of chest pains. I helped him to a cot behind the kitchen."

Claudia hopped up.

"Miss Peña," the werewolf chuckled. "It was a different cot."

Claudia wasn't taking any chances. She removed her blazer and laid it over the cot comforter before sitting again.

"Father Benedict died before I had the opportunity to summon a physician."

"A heart attack?"

"It appeared so."

"You stole his identity," Claudia accused.

"His death gave me another identity and an idea." The werewolf extended his hand to Claudia. "My given name is

Sevlow, but you may continue to call me Father Benedict, if you prefer."

She accepted his hand. Claudia expected his touch to be cold. It was not.

The padre nodded, as if he'd read her thoughts.

"Wasn't there suspicion? How do you explain not aging?" Claudia asked. "Was Seamus an orphan at St. Guinefort's?"

"In time," Sevlow said, holding up his hand.

Claudia wasn't finished. "And why don't you smell like a wet dog?"

Sevlow laughed. "Because I am a pure-breed." He stood. "If all goes well, Ms. Peña, I will answer more of your inquiries. Right now, there is a battle to plan."

"You're leaving me?" Claudia panicked. Being alone with a cordial werewolf was better than being alone. "When are you coming back?"

"As promised, I will return with your provisions and books later this afternoon. In the meantime, Hamlet will entertain you." Sevlow handed her the book he had been reading, then took a piece of stationary from atop the desk. "Do you have an author preference? Dickens? Twain? Rowling?"

Claudia had homework to do if she wanted to rescue Seamus, after she liberated herself. "Please bring me books about werewolves, if you have any."

Sevlow made himself a note. "As you wish. However, do not believe everything you read. Many legends and few truths that have been written about werewolves."

"I have another request," Claudia said, squirming a bit. "Is there a ladies' room?"

Sevlow pointed to a chamber pot against the wall.

Claudia cringed.

A tiny smile was visible on Sevlow's lips. "Some of our accommodations are more primitive than others. For that, I apologize."

"Can you tell me where I am? Where this tomb is located?" Claudia scanned the corridor looking for a door, a window, any mode of escape.

"You are far beneath St. Guinefort's. Do not bother to scream for help or attempt to flee." Sevlow held up an ornate key. "I am the lone keeper of the gate. No living soul knows the tombs exist." He placed the key back under his robe. "I must depart."

"No!" Claudia grabbed his sleeve. "Please, take me with you!"

"You will be safest here, Miss Peña." He patted her hand. "I assure you."

"Can't I be safe with you and Seamus? Or I could go home? My apartment is safe. We have a doorman. No one gets past Freddy."

"You know too much, and you feel too deeply, Miss Peña." He held her gaze. You will attempt to involve yourself in Seamus's mission if I set you free."

"I can help. I won't interfere!" Claudia begged.

"If you help, you will interfere."

Claudia realized her slip.

"Hell is about to break loose." Sevlow's voice displayed no emotion.

Claudia panicked. Her eyes welled with tears. "What if you're killed? Then how do I get out of here?"

"That is improbable, but I have made arrangements." Sevlow turned and departed without bidding her goodbye.

Claudia watched until Sevlow vanished into the darkness. She chased after him.

Sevlow opened a large wooden door framed into the stonework wall. There was a dark stairwell that led up. The door slammed and locked before Claudia could enter.

She pounded and screamed, then slid to the ground and sobbed. The ground was cold and hard. *Bucking horses, werewolves, locked doors, and chamber pots.* Claudia's body was beginning to ache from her fall. She didn't think her day could get much worse. A tap on the shoulder interrupted Claudia's pity party. She lifted her head, expecting Sevlow had returned.

"Don't cry, Miss." A little boy stood beside Claudia and held out a sack of marbles. His hands were small and gray. "I'm Simon." He set the marbles next to her. "It's ever so lonely being dead."

Chapter 9

MISSING YOU

The dilapidated 1972 Chevy C-10 had seen better days. Its rear alignment hadn't been right since Jimmy Carter left office, and the carburetor stank like a paper mill and smoked like a grill.

Seamus dialed his cell phone while driving the beater 35 mph in the expressway slow lane. Traffic whizzed past him.

"Sergeant Gaffney 20th."

"Didn't think you answered phones after 8:00 AM."

"Seamus?"

"Speaking."

"Everything OK?" The Sarge's voice had shifted into panic mode. Seamus felt a tinge of guilt. He knew it didn't take much for him to make Sergeant Gaffney's blood pressure rise and fall.

"Not exactly. I may be calling in sick tonight."

"You'd better not be sick on Monday. I need you for parade patrol. Anyway, thought running made your stomach better after a…" he hesitated.

"It does, but I've sort of got another problem." Seamus knew what was coming. He held the phone away from his ear.

"This better not be another missing-person problem!" the Sarge shouted.

Seamus pulled the steering wheel to keep the truck from tugging to the left. "Define 'missing-person' for me."

"Seamus!"

"It's not a Mickey type of problem. I don't think."

"You don't think?" the Sarge declared. "Then why are you calling?"

"I don't have anyone else to speak to about things," Seamus confessed.

"Things?" Sarge's tone was incredulous.

"Someone stole my motorcycle and my date."

Seamus had the Sarge's full attention. "A date?" mumbled the sergeant through a mouth full of antacids.

"With Claudia Peña, Alejandro Peña's sister."

"Alejandro Peña?" Gaffney echoed in a voice of disbelief. "The Bombers ballplayer, his sister?"

"Yeah, that guy. I took her out this morning for breakfast to a place up river, and she went missing." Seamus looked at his watch. "A little while ago."

"A little while ago?"

"Claudia and I were having a great time together, except when I went to the men's room somebody stole her and my motorcycle. Whoever it was left my bike helmet and a note on a matchbook."

"Where are you?" the Sarge questioned. "There's a lot of static on the line."

"I'm on my way back to the city to find Claudia and my motorcycle."

"You're walking home from up river and calling me on your cell?"

"I borrowed a vehicle," Seamus corrected.

"Define borrow," Gaffney replied.

"Someone left keys in a truck." Seamus heard the Sarge slam his office door.

"Not borrowed. Stolen! Borrowed means you had the owner's permission."

Seamus could picture Sarge rubbing his sweaty bald head, purple veins protruding from his turkey neck.

"You're a police officer!" Sergeant Gaffney yelled.

"But it's a junker," Seamus defended. "I'm sitting on springs; the radio has no knobs, and the interior's sucked its share of BO and Camels."

"That's besides the point!"

"If I accelerate up to the speed limit she sounds like a dryer full of sneakers. Listen—" Seamus hit the gas and held out the cell phone. THUMP, THUD, THUMP, THUD, THUMP!

"Seamus!" the Sarge's voice boomed across the airwaves.

"Probably used by the inn's gardener to haul lawn trash," Seamus continued. "The bed's full of tree cuttings and..." Seamus heard a horn blow and looked in his rearview mirror. Sticks and branches and grass cuttings and empty mulch bags were flying down the road behind him, causing cars to honk and swerve out of the way. He slowed back down to 35 mph. "Never mind."

"Never mind what?"

"Nothing." No sense telling the Sarge he'd littered and almost caused an accident.

"Seamus, with you it's always something!"

"Sarge, what do you know about The Cock of the Flock?" came Seamus's inquiring reply. "I know it's in the precinct."

"It's an old tavern, a historical landmark. Never any trouble there. Why?"

"I sort of remember the place being known for something besides its name."

"The Cock of the Flock was a station on the Underground Railroad."

"Oh, yeah. Built above a series of tunnels. I remember from History class. The hidden passageways were part of the slave Freedom Train."

"They were all filled in after the New City dug its subway lines and the Washington Tunnel. Why the sudden interest?"

"No reason."

"Seamus, you are up to something!"

Seamus didn't want to give Sarge any more clues to his predicament, but he still needed his boss's advice.

"What's the procedure here, Sarge? Hypothetically, if I take a girl out and she gets kidnapped, or I believe she's been kidnapped. Should I call her family and tell them? Or do I wait until I find her and then let her tell them she was abducted?"

Seamus still wasn't sure what had happened. *What if the matchbook note had nothing to do with the disappearances? What if Claudia ditched me and took my bike? She'd wear the helmet though...*

"Hypothetically?" The Sarge's voice transmitted loud and clear. "Seamus, no date of mine was ever kidnapped while I was in the bathroom, or any other time either. Weird stuff only happens to you."

90

"Because I'm a werewolf?"

"I didn't say that. I'm just saying you don't live a normal life, Seamus, and as a result, I do not live a normal life."

"But you believe me?"

"No, I don't. I find it hard to believe you have an out-of-the-blue interest in landmark taverns, that you had a breakfast date with the superstar Bomber's sister, and now she and your motorcycle have gone missing, and you've stolen a truck, and are on your way back to New City to find them." Sergeant Gaffney caught his breath. "I saw you at work this morning, Seamus. Life doesn't move that fast."

Seamus knew better. "I'm not pulling your leg, Sarge. This isn't one of my famous rubber roaches."

"That you put into my lunch box."

Seamus chuckled. "How about the crank calls?"

"Don't remind me," the sergeant snapped.

Seamus smiled and did his best Pakistani imitation. "Hello, this is Dr. Punjabi calling for Sergeant Gaffney. New City Police Department will be requiring all officers to bring stool sample to Department of Health immediately for screening of highly contagious infectious diseases."

"I'm not smiling."

Seamus could tell he was. "C'mon, Sarge. I didn't think you'd go downtown to the city health department with a zip-lock baggie full of—"

"Hey! I don't want to talk about it!"

Seamus laughed. "If you had a cellphone from this century, you'd have known it was me calling, doing a Jerky Boys."

The truck's gas gauge dipped from 1/4 to E. The vehicle began to shimmy and sputter. Seamus pressed the clutch and downshifted into second gear. Oily exhaust blew in through the open window. Seamus tried to roll up the window but the handle fell off. He was two miles from the next exit. "You've gotta admit, Sarge, it was a funny prank."

"Seamus, I think you are sitting in front of a laundromat dryer. You are waiting for your rancid running sneakers to finish an air-tumble cycle and you decided to pass the time by dialing me at work."

"Sarge, I'm—"

Sergeant Gaffney interrupted. "You are pulling my leg because you don't need sleep; you have no friends, no family, no dates, no hobbies. In other words you have nothing better to do with your free time than exercise and aggravate my bleeding ulcer!"

"Sometimes I sprout fur and howl at the moon."

"Good-bye, Seamus. I have a job to do!"

"But, Sarge, I did—"

CLICK. The phone went dead, and so did the truck.

Seamus coasted onto the grassy shoulder area of the expressway. He put the jalopy into PARK and punched the frayed dashboard. The glove box flew open.

There wasn't time to waste. Seamus tossed the key under the seat, and scooted out of the passenger-side door. He slung

Claudia's red purse across his shoulder, tucked his helmet under his arm, and reread the Cock of the Flock matchbook cover. *She didn't ditch me.* Seamus unlocked his cell phone, hit *67, and made another call.

"Riverside Inn, may I help you?"

It sounded like the waitress.

"Your gardener's truck is parked on the southbound shoulder of the expressway, between exits 47 and 46. The key's under the driver's seat and you'll need to bring a gas can—the tank's empty."

"Hello?"

"Sorry for the inconvenience. Hope you took notes. If you have any problems, this is Sergeant Ignatius Gaffney, NCPD." Seamus put his cell phone into his pocket and took off running.

Sergeant Gaffney stared at a pile of police reports on his desk. *What is that Seamus up to?* He grabbed the telephone and dialed the dispatcher. "Mildred, I want a radio car sent to The Cock of the Flock. Tell 'em to keep out of sight.... No, nothing in particular.... I just want an activity account—who's coming and going.... Right.... No police response, just a report... Thanks." The Sarge hung up and returned to his paperwork.

Twenty minutes later his phone rang.

"Hello." Sarge reached for his pen and note pad. "Mildred, what d'ya got?... An African-American guy on a red BMW motorcycle... Wasn't wearing a helmet... Drove the bike into a shed behind the building... No, I don't want them to do anything.

In fact, tell the officers they can go…. I have the information I need… Right, I'll take it from here. Thanks, Mildred." Sergeant Gaffney put on his hat and headed out the door.

Chapter 10

LEADER OF THE PACK

Sevlow's werewolf pack lived in a windowless cluster of basement rooms beneath the Cock of the Flock tavern. The youthful trio left their distinct mark on the den, a.k.a.: playhouse, frat house, out house.

TJ, the most senior pack member, returned from his appointed errand. He loped into the subterranean werewolf den wearing a body-hugging leather vest, torn jeans, and a relaxed smile. He parked his strapping mass on the ratty sofa.

"Toweled the bike down and slid her into the old ice shed. Not a scratch on her." TJ hurled a soiled pillow at a muscular tattooed Asian teen across the room.

Dragon leapt and met the projectile with a snapping mid-air side thrust kick. The pillow detonated on impact, releasing a downy cloud.

"Damn, Jackie Chan!" TJ marveled. "Your fly through the air soaring sumo stunts amaze me every time!"

"Confucius say, the superior man is modest in his speech, but exceeds in his actions." Dragon bowed before brushing a wad of feathers out of his spiky bleached brindled hair. "You like the bike?"

"Who wouldn't drool over a Beemer K 1300 XP? I had no problem taking her up to 90 in a 65. Perfectly sized. Monstrously exciting, with enough raw power to shock."

"Thanks for the review, TV guy," Dragon teased. "Do you

really remember every movie, sitcom, and commercial you've ever seen?"

"Yep," TJ replied. "Go ahead; quiz me."

Dragon rolled his eyes.

"Any television show that's been on in the last 50 years," TJ challenged.

"*The Munsters*." Dragon said. "What type of pet does Eddie keep under the stairs?"

"Man, that's a gimme." TJ waved his hand in mock disgust. "Spot, a fire-breathing dragon. Think of a hard one; take your time. Police boy's got a long run ahead of him."

"Sure Seamus will find us?"

"Believe me. He wants his shiny bike back." TJ tossed a book of matches to his den mate. "I left a calling card, one of these with a little note inside."

"Clever," Dragon congratulated.

TJ blew on his fingernails and buffed them on his chest. "Sevlow's idea."

"What's Seamus like in person?"

TJ shrugged. "Solid, a little taller than you, he has our sweet tooth and dog funk. But unlike you and me, Seamus has found himself a girlfriend, an equestrian Barbie who is no she wolf."

"A mortal? Maybe she's stink blind." Dragon held his nose. "We should get out more in the daylight hours," Dragon lamented.

"What's stopping you?" TJ replied. "Maybe you should wear something besides neon tiger pajama pants."

"They're Zubaz." Dragon plopped down on the sofa beside TJ. POOF! A cloud of dust shot into the air.

"Damn, Captain Underpants!" TJ waved his hand in front of his face and pretended to choke.

Dragon pulled an open bag of crunched Chocolate Cookie Supremes out from beneath the soiled cushion.

TJ helped himself to a fistful of Dragon's double-stuffed cookie crumbs and grabbed the TV remote off the littered coffee table. "Where's Mighty Mouse?"

"Said he was going to his room to play video games." Dragon scratched the giant fire-breathing winged serpent inked across his shirtless hairless chest. "We should leave the kid out of this mission. All that mind-game stuff might be too dangerous."

"Mighty Mouse ain't a pup anymore. He's like a hundred, and he's been a werewolf way longer than you," TJ reminded, clicking through the cable channels.

"A kid and now a rookie werewolf," Dragon took a fistful of darts off the two-legged end table and aimed them at a torn oil painting across the room. All four hit their mark.

"There'll be enough action for everyone," TJ said. "If Sevlow wants Seamus to join this mission, so be it."

"The superior man seeks in himself what the small man seeks in others."

"You know, your Oriental wisdom sometimes gets on my nerves. Speak in Occidental, Grasshopper."

Dragon let out a long belch.

"Man!" TJ yelled. "My ears are ringing from that one!"

97

"Translation: Our pack doesn't need any more leaders. What if Seamus comes in here and wants to run the show?"

"Quit whining, Stinky."

"I still don't understand how come Sevlow didn't approach Seamus, tell him what's going down, instead of having you steal the bike and leading him here."

"Seamus was kept in the dark since being turned," TJ reminded. "Sevlow wants to give him a little taste of dealing with our type for a change."

"Confucius say, have no friends not equal to yourself."

TJ moaned.

"Seamus wins medals kicking butt in the mortal world. We could kick mortal butt in our sleep." Dragon shook the last of the cookie crumbs into his mouth. "If we slept."

"What's your problem, Oscar the Grouch? This ain't a competition. Sevlow says Seamus is ready to join the pack. End of discussion." TJ checked his watch.

"Even if Seamus follows your clue and finds us here." Dragon tossed the empty Tollhouse bag behind the sofa. "What makes you think Seamus wants to join us?"

"Same reason you, Mighty Mouse, and I have hung with Sevlow all these years, Bro." TJ threw his huge feet up on the coffee table. It collapsed. "We're one big happy dysfunctional family *and* a winning team."

"TJ, Dragon!" Mighty Mouse yelled from the hall. A ginger-haired boy riding a skateboard skidded to a noisy stop against the wolf den doorway. "Someone's snooping around out back by the shed! Hurry!"

Sergeant Gaffney used his handkerchief to wipe away a half-century worth of grime and pigeon guano from the glass pane on the old ice shed. Through a squint and a flashlight beam he could make out the shape of a motorcycle in the shadowy dimness. Sarge checked the shed entries. The door was chained and padlocked. Both windows were barred. He gave a glance to his left and right. The dead-end alley behind the Cock of the Flock was deserted. So Gaffney thought.

"You got a warrant, Kojak? Or does the Patriot Act cover your trespassing butt on private property?"

TJ and Dragon appeared and blocked the only alley exit. They weren't the welcoming committee.

"Hey, TJ, looks like Seamus called the cops on us," Dragon said.

"Now don't it seem that way, Dragon?" TJ kicked an empty beer can.

Sergeant Gaffney removed his service revolver from its holster. Before he could strike a defensive pose, a bare foot appeared and punted the gun from his grip.

Mighty Mouse caught the .32 and dashed out of view.

"What the?" Sarge stammered.

"I wouldn't have pegged Sullivan for a stool pigeon," TJ sized up the Sergeant. "Figured he'd fight his own battles."

"Let's get some rope and lock him in the shed until we're finished with business," Dragon suggested.

The Sarge took a step back. "How do you two know Seamus?"

"We don't," TJ said. "And your being here complicates our first meeting." He advanced and reached for the Sarge's handcuffs.

Sergeant Gaffney attempted to block TJ's massive arm. It would have been easier to halt a speeding iron girder.

The big man smiled.

Sergeant Gaffney pulled his nightstick and lunged.

TJ overpowered the Sarge with ease and incapacitated him with his own law enforcement gear. "Keep still, Starsky. I'm not gonna hurt you."

I smell wet dog. Gaffney raised his knee and connected with TJ's groin.

"Man!" TJ tossed the Sarge like a rag doll against the shed door, wrists bound, dirty hanky shoved into his mouth. "Now look what you made me do."

"Pick on someone your own size!" came a voice from behind.

Dragon and TJ spun around.

Seamus approached, still sporting Claudia's red purse, and a helmet tucked beneath his right arm.

"Your bag's cute, but it clashes with your helmet," TJ ragged.

Before the big man could utter another wisecrack, Seamus clenched his fist and threw a staggering left jab that connected, snapping TJ's startled head back with the force of the strike. Off balance, TJ tripped on the rutted concrete. He fell like an axed redwood—hard. He was dazed for a moment.

Dragon circled, like a vulture before a feast.

Sarge spit out his gag. "Seamus!" he warned.

Seamus grabbed Dragon's foot mid thrust and twisted it like a loose doorknob. Bones cracked and splintered.

A single gun blast rang out across the alley. Seamus grabbed his gut and fell to the ground. "Shot for the second time in one day," Seamus moaned.

The Sarge could see Seamus's eyes flutter and roll back into his head. He could hear the sound of flesh stretching and bones creaking as Seamus's wounded body bucked, writhed, and sprouted fur and fangs.

An instant later Seamus was transformed.

Seamus the brawny black werewolf hopped up. He was nose-to-nose-to-nose with two other werewolves, one massive and mahogany, one brawny and brindle.

"Holy Smokes!" Sergeant Gaffney shrieked. He inch-wormed himself across the alley and underneath the rancid garbage dumpster. He parked his rear on something cold, wet, putrid, and squishy—he didn't bother to investigate the source. The Sarge had a safe unsanitary ringside view of the smoldering dogfight.

Fur commenced flying.

Seamus the werewolf was the same as Seamus the boxer: an opportunistic scrapper. He gnawed and ripped and scratched at any ear and lip and dewclaw that brushed past his furious fangs.

Although not as powerful as the mahogany or as agile as the brindle werewolf, Seamus's advantage was speed, a seething temper, and endurance. He bobbed and weaved his way through the furry wrangle. The three werewolves raced around the alley, tumbling and slashing. Seamus had the duo beside the shed. He dug his paws in and body-butted the brindle while gnawing at the mahogany's face. Both managed to slip free of Seamus's advance. They retreated, with the new aggressor nipping at their heels in hot pursuit.

The vicious tussle continued behind the ice shed, out of Sergeant Gaffney's view. He could hear yelping and growling and snarling. The Sarge feared for his man, until Seamus reappeared, still full of vigor. The alley brawl winner hadn't been determined.

Sergeant Gaffney found himself coaching from the corner. "Those dogs took your bike and your girl! The big one's getting tired! Chase him!"

Seamus ran TJ down and tackled him.

"Lookout behind you, Seamus! The brindle is…"

Seamus grabbed hold of Dragon.

"Way to fight!" cheered the Sarge. "Go for the underbelly!"

Seamus tore a hunk of spotted flesh. Dragon yelped but did not retreat, blood oozed from a gaping wound. His sights were on Seamus. Seamus kept an eye on the angry brindle as he shadowed the big werewolf again. TJ was panting hard and limping. Seamus cornered him at the back of the alley. The green-eyed wolf snarled and stared. The mahogany werewolf steadied himself—he was ailing, but didn't appear ready to roll over and play dead.

The brindle moved in closer.

"You're about to get double teamed!" the Sarge cautioned.

Before either Dragon or TJ could spring, both were thrust into the air by a force so stealth it seemed invisible. Seamus crouched low in a protective pose. A huge white werewolf with steely blue eyes loomed in front of him. The leader of the pack morphed back into a man.

"Father Benedict?" Sergeant Gaffney asked in disbelief.

Seamus's vision was beginning to blur. In the darkening haze he caught a glimpse of Claudia, floating in her sphere of luminescence. She was waving, shouting something he could not hear. Seamus tried to remain conscious. It was futile. He went down for the count with Father Benedict's voice echoing in his ears.

"Seamus, you are worthy."

Chapter 11

LOST BOYS

"Seamus, help me!"

The sound of Claudia's own dream-scream awoke her with a start. She took a quick look around, hoping her kidnapping had also been a nightmare. It wasn't. Claudia was still in the cold tomb prison. She threw her head back against the huge downy pillow and groaned. "I'm still here, and evidently, Seamus has met his pack."

Simon the dead boy hovered beside Claudia's bed holding his bag of marbles and looking concerned.

"You had a bad dream, Miss." He reached for her hand.

Claudia felt a brief puff of cold air. "Don't worry, Simon." She smiled. "It's not the first time." Claudia patted the end of her cot. "Sit."

Simon grinned and obeyed.

Claudia remembered playing a game of marbles, then another, and another. She remembered asking Simon if he minded coming back later. The stress of the day, the previous night, Claudia fell asleep exhausted.

"Father came," Simon said, pointing to a short table against the wall.

"The white-haired man brought supplies?"

Simon nodded. "When you were sleeping."

"Can he see you, too?"

"No, Miss," Simon replied. "Only you."

Claudia hopped up to investigate. She dug through the wicker picnic basket. There were three loaves of fresh bread wrapped in cotton dishtowels, a sack containing oranges and apples, a waxy wedge of hard cheese, a tin of dried meat, and a small bottle of greenish liquid. The cork had been loosened; she opened it and took a sniff. "Garlic and olive oil. Wow, the padre took care packing this feast." Claudia was impressed.

Next to the basket were linen napkins and eating utensils. He also provided a flashlight, extra batteries, and a first-aid kit. There was a case of bottled water beneath the table. The padre had placed a small plastic washbasin, a facecloth, a hand towel, and three rolls of toilet paper atop the case.

Claudia remembered the chamber pot. *Disgusting.* At the corner of the supply table was a burlap satchel. It contained books. Claudia emptied the contents. FAMOUS WITCH AND WEREWOLF TRIALS, FANGS AND PHANTOMS, MOONLIGHT AND MAYHEM. There were a dozen werewolf books, new and ancient, hardcover and paperback, some with bookmarks between pages.

There was a handwritten note pinned to the satchel.

Dear Miss Peña,

Here are the werewolf books you requested. I have marked those accounts I believe you will find most fascinating. Nearly all of the tales on these pages are fictional. However, some fact has made its way into the fantasy. Regrettably, I do not have sufficient time to separate the truths from falsehoods. I promise to

shed more light on this matter at another time. I hope
you will be comfortable during my leave, and your
provisions and surroundings adequate.
Respectfully,
Sevlow

Claudia grabbed the top book and a hunk of warm sourdough bread. She plopped back down on her cot.

"Please read me a story," Simon begged, hovering beside her, sporting a persuasive pout.

"Simon, these stories may be too scary for you." Claudia heard herself and laughed at the absurdity of the statement. *How can a story frighten a ghost?* "OK, Simon, I'll read to you. But first tell me why you're still here. Why you haven't passed to the other side? You've seen the bright white light. Haven't you?"

Simon nodded. "Yes, Miss."

"You don't have to stay here on earth." Claudia knew from her parents that earth-bound spirits were souls with unfinished business. Visitor spirits were a different breed. They traveled between the light and the living.

"I want to wait for my brother." Simon's eyes teared. "Wait for Benjamin."

Claudia wished she could hug the gray-skinned little boy. She attempted to pat Simon's ginger curls. Her hand slipped through him; she felt a current of cold air.

Simon didn't seem to notice that he'd been touched. He fumbled with his bag of marbles.

"Simon, I'm guessing you died many years ago." Claudia fluffed her pillow and snuggled herself against it. She took another bite of bread.

"I'm six."

"You're six, a big boy, and very brave to stay here so long to wait for your brother. Is Benjamin an old man now?"

Simon shook his head "no." He held up eight fingers.

"Benjamin's eight?" questioned Claudia. She surveyed Simon's ghost clothing. His zipperless brown knickers fastened with a rope belt. His shirt was pleated and collarless. His shoes were stitched leather with four side buttons instead of laces. "Maybe your brother has passed on and you don't know it."

"Benjamin plays with big dogs," Simon said. He pointed to the cover of the book Claudia was holding.

"These are werewolves, Simon, not dogs."

"Big, big dogs!" Simon stretched his arms wide.

"I guess you could say they're big dogs." Claudia smiled. Simon was adorable, in an ashy creepy sort of way. She was glad to have the company, until she could find a way out of her predicament.

Simon stretched out on the bed beside her.

Claudia examined the book's cover more closely, FRENCH WEREWOLVES IN PARIS. The jacket contained a drawing of two werewolves standing on their hind legs in front of the Eiffel Tower. They were obviously a couple; they were holding paws. The male sported a blue beret. He was smoking a cigarette. The female wore a pink bow and a chunky necklace. Blood dripped from their fangs and mangled bodies lay at their feet. A full moon illuminated the cartoon carnage. Claudia turned the book over. "Simon, how about I tell you a story instead?"

The pack was back in the wolf den nursing their scuffle wounds. Mighty Mouse scurried between Dragon and TJ, bringing towels and ice packs. Seamus leaned shirtless against the wall. His right arm was in a makeshift sling; his chest displayed an assortment of scrapes and bruises.

Sevlow handed the Sarge a bottled water. "Please excuse the surroundings. My tenants have a high threshold for stench and squalor."

Sergeant Gaffney took the cold container and held it against his red wrist. He was sitting on a wobbly folding chair, which had been decorated with kid stickers and magic marker scribbles.

Sevlow observed Sarge's outfit, a borrowed pair of Zubaz and a dirty undershirt. "I apologize, Sergeant Gaffney for your ordeal, and for your ruined uniform. It was not my intention to have us meet again in this manner."

"To go too far is as bad as to fall short," Dragon groaned, holding a bloody towel over his torn abdomen.

"Belated wisdom," TJ replied.

"I'm OK, but shouldn't he see a doctor?" Sergeant Gaffney asked, pointing to Dragon. "All three of them probably ought to get checked out."

"Their wounds will heal before long." Sevlow inspected Dragon's gash. "The subcutaneous layer has already begun to mend itself." He placed a clean damp rag over the injury. "The tattoo won't be marred."

"I didn't think werewolves could be hurt," Sarge declared. "Seamus has been shot and burned and—"

"By mortals." Sevlow explained. "Until this afternoon Seamus had not encountered another supernatural." Sevlow resumed his rounds. He examined Seamus.

"So they can be killed?" the Sarge asked.

"Not exactly, but it is impossible for a human to kill a werewolf," Sevlow replied.

"What about Lon Chaney Jr.?" Sarge recalled. "A silver bullet stopped him. Or was it a stake through the heart? Didn't he play both the Wolfman and Dracula?"

Seamus may have been mending on the outside, but his temper was still smoldering. He spoke up and changed the monster movie subject. "TJ, I'm going to ask you one more time. Where's Claudia?"

"And I'm going to tell you for the last time, Rin Tin Tin. I have no clue. Maybe Tonto brought her horse by the restaurant and they rode off into the sunset together." TJ stopped mid laugh and held his ribs. "All I did was swipe your bike."

Seamus took an aggressive step forward.

Sevlow pressed him back against the wall. "Miss Peña is in my care," Sevlow said without a trace of emotion in his voice. "She is safe and will remain so until the mission we are about to embark upon is completed."

"You kidnapped Claudia?" Seamus could feel his temper rise; his fists clenched. He stared into Sevlow's familiar blue eyes, expecting to see his fury returned. However, he saw only benevolence staring back at him.

Sevlow held Seamus's gaze. "Twelve floors is a long way down," the leader reminded. His tone was kind, but firm.

Seamus understood. His body relaxed. He looked away, embarrassed. It all made sense. *My crazy daredevil stunts, I should be dead.* Father Benedict had long ago earned Seamus's undying love, respect, and gratitude. Now Seamus was forever indebted to the white werewolf, too.

Sevlow nodded at Seamus, as if he'd heard his thoughts, as if to say the night at the construction site would remain their secret. Sevlow adjusted the sling on Seamus's shoulder. "It was obvious to me this morning that Miss Peña has won your affections."

Seamus's thoughts shifted from himself to Claudia. He looked away. "Sir, I couldn't forgive myself if anything happened to her."

"For that reason, Miss Peña has been sequestered until our mission is complete." Sevlow removed a rolled piece of parchment paper from atop the table. "The time has come. I require your werewolf assistance."

Seamus felt an odd sort of relief. He longed to see Claudia again, sooner rather than later. But he was also excited by the idea of having a chance to use his werewolf powers as they were intended. It was a guy thing, a case of romance vs. warfare, *Pride and Prejudice* or *Gladiator*. If given the choice of dinner with a supermodel or a chance to quarterback for the home team, most guys would pick the pigskin, especially if the supermodel could be impounded until after the game. Seamus figured he'd have his Claudia and his combat too. "What about Claudia's family, her brother and parents? Won't they worry?" Seamus wasn't a total jock.

"Miss Peña's parents died long ago, and her brother left for Bean Town this afternoon. I follow the Bombers," Sevlow said.

"You don't miss a beat," Seamus replied.

"The superior man seeks knowledge before action, while the fool acts in haste and invites defeat," an energetic voice came from the sofa.

"Well, lookie here. Confucius is feeling better." TJ remarked.

Dragon checked his wound. There was a pink scar where the gash had been. His Dragon tail had reappeared. He shoved the towel under the sofa. "Who's hungry?"

Seamus removed his sling and flexed and twisted his arm. His shoulder had repaired itself. He raised his hand. "I could go for donuts."

"Hot fudge sundae," TJ chimed. "I'm so hungry I might hijack a Mr. Frosty truck. Mighty Mouse, go get your Halloween stash."

Mighty Mouse ran off to fetch.

"Camaraderie via confectionery consumption," Sevlow observed.

The mood in the room lightened.

TJ extended his hand to the Sarge, who shook it. "Sorry, man."

"Me too," Dragon called from the sofa. "We don't get out much. Sevlow says our manners are atrocious."

"Yeah, the Sarge tried to send me to obedience school too," Seamus added.

Mighty Mouse offered Seamus candy from an orange pumpkin bucket.

Seamus helped himself to a handful of stale treats. "But this little guy! Didn't anyone teach him not to play with guns?" Seamus tried to grab hold of Mighty Mouse, who scooted away in a flash.

Mighty Mouse ran to Dragon for protection. He peeked over the back of the sofa and stuck his tongue at Seamus.

"Why would you turn a little kid?" Seamus asked Sevlow.

"I turned Mighty Mouse," TJ confessed.

"We have the power to turn a mortal too?" Seamus asked.

"You've got a lot learn," Dragon said.

"New City suffered a Tuberculosis outbreak just before the turn of the century," Sevlow replied. "Our school was hit hard by the disease,"

"That would be late 1890's, for those of you who aren't used to werewolf time," TJ explained. "Centuries sorta run together after a while."

"Yes," Sevlow continued. "In 1898, Benjamin's brother and five other of my boys succumbed to the epidemic. TJ took pity on the child."

"He was dying in my arms. I'm no doctor, but I did what I could to save him. A fang to the heart!" TJ growled before snatching Mighty Mouse off the sofa and tussling him like a rag doll.

The boy squealed with delight.

"And we've been paying the price of perpetual puppy ever since!" TJ roared.

"TJ's a softie," Dragon said. "He's been banished from the orphanage."

"TJ and Huang, I mean, Dragon," Sevlow corrected himself. "And of course, Seamus, are werewolves of my creation."

"I know Seamus's story," Sarge said. "Well, at least the part he's told me."

Sevlow smiled at Seamus and remained silent.

Sarge pointed at Dragon and TJ. "Are they also from St. Guinefort's?"

"Nope. TJ's the former president's son," Dragon said. "TJ's dad had a mistress."

"I'm gonna guess you're Bill's kid," Seamus quipped. "But you look nothing like Monica."

"Spaz! You're two centuries off." TJ hit Seamus with a candy bar. "History doesn't mention me because the old dude's farm book didn't list a child named Tom, because my mama said I was born a freeman, not a piece of property. On my 18th birthday I left home and joined the cause."

"I was given orders to assist the Underground Railroad," Sevlow continued. "The Cock of the Flock became a station, a safe house."

"Whose orders?" Sarge questioned.

"We are hounds of the gods!" Dragon howled.

Sergeant Gaffney looked confused.

"Without gods and werewolves to combat Beelzebub's stinking bedlam, this world would suck even worse," TJ added.

"Beelzebub?" the Sarge asked. "The Old Testament devil had something to do with bringing slavery to America?"

"Good and bad go by many names, and take on as many forms," Sevlow explained. "TJ was turned to aid with the escort. I required assistance providing safe passage to the freemen."

"The truth would blow your Sunday school mind," TJ added. "This wolf didn't lose any of his flock."

"Fall of Saigon." Dragon announced his own origin. "Lost my entire family during an air raid."

"Operation Get the Hell Out," TJ recalled. "Sevlow turned Huang, the 16-year-old karate kid with the giant dragon tattoo. He became our teenage insider. There were scared orphaned children to move. Dragon speaks English and *Canh Chua Ca Loc*."

"Snake and mullet stew," Dragon translated. "I didn't eat that sh—"

Sevlow interrupted the banter. "As you may have gathered, Sergeant Gaffney, werewolf missions are not confined to New City."

"Lost boys will travel." TJ shoved a wad of red licorice into his mouth.

"However, this mission is local. Sevlow unrolled his parchment. It was a diagram of the city. "I wanted to give Seamus ample opportunity to adjust to his altered state." Sevlow gestured towards the sergeant. "This has also given you, Sergeant Gaffney, time to acquaint yourself with the challenges of fostering a werewolf."

"Hey Sarge, sounds like you're going to be asked to help out," Seamus said. "And you thought your best cops-and-robbers days were behind you!"

"Really?" Sarge threw back his shoulders. "You need my help?"

"Yes," Sevlow replied. "This mission will require assistance from law enforcement."

"I don't know, Sarge," Seamus teased. "Might mean you'll have to do something more dangerous than sit behind a desk and cut your toenails."

"Will the assistance," Gaffney hesitated. "Ah, jeopardize my pension?"

"I will need you to make a phone call," Sevlow said.

"A phone call?" Sergeant Gaffney appeared relieved. "I can do that."

"Very good." Sevlow highlighted an area on the map. "I believed you would be agreeable," Sevlow pointed to the marked location. "This is a section of your precinct, Sergeant Gaffney. When I give the command, I will need you to call the mayor. He must stop the M and G trains from running beneath Midtown Gardens Park."

Sergeant Gaffney's face lost its ruddy hue.

Seamus howled. "The Sarge is about to lose his pension!"

Chapter 12

DYNAMIC DUO

The New City Chronicle's office was deserted. Every reporter worth their weight in stale coffee grounds knew hanging around the city bureau on weekends was for suck-ups and desperate has-beens. No real news happened on Saturday and Sunday.

Lyman Newlin sat at his cubicle desk reading last week's funny papers and chewing on an unlit cigar. The newspaper building was a smoke-free workplace. Lyman had once been a player at the *Chronicle*, a journalist celebrity. His correspondent career hit a Pulitzer-mention high the year Saturday Night Live took to the late night airwaves and police detective Hank Scorpio blew the whistle on the NCPD's rampant corruption. Lyman snagged an exclusive interview with Scorpio and broke the story first on the front page of *The New City Chronicle*. *60 Minutes'* Harry Reasoner and *The Tonight Show's* Johnny Carson came calling. Lyman did the talk show circuit for weeks. Everyone in America wanted to know how Lyman Newlin had landed the New City story of the decade. Lyman still sometimes wondered himself. But fame is fickle and fleeting. Despite a best selling book and hit movie that followed, few people remembered Hank Scorpio or the reporter who risked his neck to tattle the tale—the bureaucratic backlash, the death threats. *Those were the days!* Five mayors, thirty pounds, two dirty divorces, and a quadruple bypass later, Lyman was a birthday shy of Social Security senior. He yearned for another sensational scoop to launch him into permanent retirement. It was Lyman's dream to revitalize his reputation and go out with a bang, but the NCPD wasn't cooperating. The department had been clean for ages and the officers were behaving themselves—no prisoner abuse scandals or racial tensions. The only semi-stimulating story Lyman could generate in the last few years featured a young hero cop named Seamus Sullivan and his mysterious big black dog. For a while Lyman banked on the hunch there was a huge news story there, somewhere. But now that Sullivan was on park patrol things were quiet, no more courageous escapades. Lyman decided he'd been mistaken. *Best to let sleeping dogs lie.*

Lyman Newlin was startled from his comics by a commotion in the hallway. He could hear Jesus the janitor arguing with someone. Someone with a deep, throaty, smoker's hack, like that sound a cat makes just before it throws up. Lyman set down his cigar and waddled off to investigate. In the hall, Lyman found Jesus backed against the water cooler. He'd lost his mop to a 4'11" Gollum-voiced granny who looked willing and able to swing with an audacious vengeance.

"I gotta gripe with the police department and you ain't gonna stop me from making a citizen's complaint!" she rasped, poking the mop handle beneath the bewildered janitor's chin.

"No speak English," he stammered.

"Liar! 'No speak English' *is* English!" she snarled, pressing on the wooden pole until her captive's eyes bulged and his knees buckled.

Lyman to the rescue! He kicked the janitor's muck bucket and sent it sailing into the back of the woman's stumpy little legs. She dropped the mop on impact and tumbled forward.

The frightened cleaning man saw his opening. He darted to his left, into the men's bathroom. The lavatory door lock clicked.

The wound-tight woman bounced off the water cooler and landed like a zapped roach on her back. She glared up at the bucket kicker, limbs wiggling.

Their eyes met.

There was something mesmerizing about the aged pit bull's intent glare. It commanded attention. Lyman was afraid to move.

"You're that Scorpio reporter, Newlin," she said, after giving Lyman a long once-over. "You got old and fat."

He nodded in agreement.

She rolled out of the damp spot and righted herself unassisted. "I still read your column," she growled through a trace grin.

Lyman could smell tobacco and garlic on her breath.

"Clarabella Stella, but you can call me Bella." She dusted off her damp polyester pants suit. "You write good."

It had been an eternity, but Bella recognized Lyman and then uttered the magic words: *You write good.* Lyman felt thirty years younger and a foot taller. Flattery also impacted his vision. Lyman couldn't help but notice the feisty woman's two attributes. *That soft combed perm, those gleaming white dentures.* Lyman's 5'5" ego fell for Bella Stella like his heart was a mob informant, and she was a sack of quick-drying cement. He tilted his neck and tried to look cool. "What can I do you for?" The new and improved Lyman Newlin rolled his shoulders and replied in his best tough guy voice.

"My son's been missing since last night and the cops won't put out an Amber alert!" Mama Stella bellowed. "So what if Mickey's 37? The mook is still my kid!"

"How about a missing person? You should file a report."

"The cops say I gotta wait two days." Bella clenched her fists and snarled, "I think there's a conspiracy, and I aim to get to the bottom of it."

Lyman knew she meant business. He came down from his tiptoes and took a step backwards. "It *is* police procedure to give an adult missing person 48 hours to show before a report can be filed," he said with caution. The mop was in Bella's grabbing range. Intimidated or not, the flattered journalist couldn't let himself disappoint a fan. "But I might be able to help you out."

"Thought so." Mama Stella took a scrap of paper from her pocket. "I found this in Mickey's room." She handed the torn sheet of loose leaf paper to Lyman.

He read it aloud, "Cock of the Flock, 8:30."

"The stupid mook was probably doing gay porno," she speculated.

Lyman stifled a laugh. "It's an old tavern, near the park." He handed her back the scrap. "Maybe the bartender remembers seeing your son, Mickey. I can ask some questions. If you want to come back to my desk, I'll make a few calls. Gimme a description and any other information you might remember. Was your son supposed to meet anyone? What was he wearing? What was he driving?" Lyman kicked into reporter mode. He could tell it was impressing Bella.

"Forget the phone." Mama Stella yanked Lyman by his frayed blazer. "My car's double-parked outside. Lead the way!"

Lyman was dragged to the elevator before he could protest. He patted his pants pocket. He had his wallet and keys. Missing persons wasn't his niche, but Lyman figured driving around town with Bella Stella beat spending another lonely Saturday afternoon sucking on a soggy cigar.

He pressed the DOWN button. "OK, this is now an official newspaper investigation, *New City Chronicle* business," Lyman said. "There's a protocol that must be followed. It's mandatory that the authorized correspondent be in charge of—"

"Shut-up," Bella interrupted. The floor bell dinged. Mama Stella was giving the orders. She pushed Lyman into the empty elevator and punched button L. "I drive and you ask the questions when we get to the Flocking Cock."

She's my kinda woman. Lyman smiled. The doors slid closed. The Otis descended nine floors to the lobby below.

Bella's silver Pacer circled the block twice. Parking places were few and far between in New City and Mama Stella's stunted arms were only capable of right turns. The moon buggy didn't come equipped with power steering.

On the second revolution Lyman spotted a familiar figure in the alley behind the Cock of the Flock. It was Seamus Sullivan. "Stop!" Lyman cried.

Bella slammed on the breaks. Lyman fell off the bench seat and hit his chin on the dash. The lap belt had malfunctioned.

"You see Mickey?" Bella handed Lyman a first communion picture of Mickey and peered over the wheel, surveying the sidewalk. "He's still got the same face."

Lyman rubbed his sore stubble. "No, it's not him. It's a cop. I'm wondering why?" Lyman quieted when he saw Father X. Francis Benedict *and* Sergeant Gaffney join Seamus in the alley.

Gaffney was wearing neon pajama pants and a soiled undershirt. Father Benedict unlocked a shed. Seamus wheeled out his motorcycle and hopped aboard.

Lyman's reporter radar clicked into red alert. "Very interesting…"

"What?" Bella demanded.

"We've got a hero cop, his Sergeant out of uniform, and a priest who runs an orphanage all loitering together in an alley behind an old tavern. Something's going on at the Cock of the Flock."

"Maybe Mickey's mixed up in it too. He's always up to no good."

Lyman watched as Seamus put on his helmet and started up his bike. "Pull into the bus stop; don't let him see me."

Bella veered right and drove over the yellow curb.

"A bus is coming. I gotta get out of this lane."

"Hold on a minute."

Seamus drove his red Beemer out of the alley, looked both ways and gunned it towards the park.

"Follow that motorcycle," Lyman instructed.

Mama Stella hit the gas, cut-off the uptown #27, and sent a cluster of straphangers tumbling. Bella was two vehicles behind when Seamus turned left onto the Midtown Gardens thoroughfare.

Lyman grabbed hold of the steering wheel. "One, two, three —left!" It took all his turning might, but moon buggy made the quick turn and kept Seamus in sight. "Oooo Eeee!" Lyman was back in the game.

Chapter 13

FOLLOW ME

Seamus took a quick left onto the Midtown Gardens thoroughfare. He didn't notice the silver Pacer rolling in two cars behind him. At the south exit of the park Seamus veered onto the Eastside Expressway, merged into the speed lane, and gunned it towards exit #3, Round Island. Seamus was headed home.

Round Island was now a man-made peninsula, thanks to millions of tons of New City landfill deliberately deposited into the channel Mother Nature designed to separate the adjacent landmasses. The solid strait was then paved and renamed Highway 99. Once upon a time, the tiny barrier island was a summer spot where New Citiers came to swim, sun, and ride the world's third largest wooden roller coaster. That was before the great fire of '74, a three-alarm blaze that wiped out Island Amusement Park and most of its bordering beach bungalows.

The island changed hungry developer hands many times over the years. Grandiose plans for towering condominiums had come and gone. More deals were in the works when an anonymous investor paid an substantial sum for the forty acre round, and then left the parcel untouched. Seamus figured it was a conservationist calm before the bulldozer storm.

In the meantime, few original Round Island dwellings and only one resident remained. Seamus rented one of the six enduring bungalows scattered along the abandoned shore. The nameless landlord let him have it cheap. It didn't make a difference to

Seamus that the tiny house had electricity but neither heat nor hot water. Werewolves are impervious to temperature extremes; their bodies stay at a constant 101.5 degrees.

What attracted Seamus to the place was the island's serene seclusion and pirate past. The former Native American inhabitants called it Narrioch Island. The isle's round shape kept its sandy beach bathed in sunlight all day, and moonlight all night, making it a *narrioch*, or "land without shadows." In the 17th and 18th centuries, Narrioch Island was a favorite hideout for British and French buccaneers on their way back to Europe from plundering Spaniard vessels in the West Indies. The perimeter of the island was easy to patrol, and ships could hide in the deep, sheltered creek that fed into the ocean strait.

Father Benedict used to tell the children amazing accounts of pirates who sought refuge on the island. Young Seamus enjoyed hearing the headmaster's animated tales of daring sea battles and hidden treasures, still undiscovered. Seamus would lie in bed at night and fantasize about being a member of the brave buccaneer squad. *Finally, I'm part of a team.* His thoughts shifted to the upcoming mission as he took his exit.

The same train of thought made him wonder how Claudia was dealing with her confinement. Seamus could picture her face: beautiful, intent, probably planning an escape. His undead heart raced and his stomach fluttered. One thought led to another. Seamus fantasized about Claudia as he drove along the rutted road that led home, her smile, her curvy body, her warm soft kiss. Breakfast seemed like ages ago.

Seamus shut his mind and pushed his longing down, to the place inside of him that could forget, if only for a while, then stopped his motorcycle in front of a small, whitewashed cottage set back from the beach road among the tall grasses and reeds. A wide wooden walkway led through the sand to the front door of the bungalow. The house didn't have a garage. Sand and sea air took its toll on paint and chrome. Seamus rolled his motorcycle through the front door, and into the kitchen-dining area. He planted the kickstand on a scrap of remnant rug. The tidy dual room consisted of a bedroom-living area along side the kitchen-dining area. A windowless bathroom was separated from view by two sidewalls and a makeshift curtain. The furnishings were sparse but adequate.

Seamus removed a canister from the cabinet and sprinkled two pellets of Betta Morsels into a tank on the kitchen counter. "Dinner time, Bluebeard." A sapphire Siamese fighting fish wiggled his frilly tail and feasted. Seamus checked the tank's heating apparatus and thermometer. "82 degrees. Warmer than the ice shower I'm about to take." He kicked off his shoes and unbuttoned his soiled shirt. Seamus opened the freezer and removed a tub of rocky road ice cream. A silver spoon protruded from the center of the frosty mound. He wolfed down a large scoop. "Might be gone for a few days," Seamus said with a mouth full. He gobbled a second helping before putting the ice cream container back into the freezer. Seamus dropped another pellet into Bluebeard's bowl.

The frilly fish gorged.

Seamus stripped to his boxers and dumped his dirty clothes

into a basket next to the opened sofa bed. He yanked a duffel down from atop a tall bookcase that doubled as a dresser. Seamus packed clean underwear, socks, jeans, and two shirts. He tossed the zipped bag onto the open futon and slipped behind the bathroom curtain.

The *shhhhh* of the running shower and another mental image of Claudia in the buff prevented Seamus's canine ears from hearing an approaching car, and the bickering going on inside of it.

"Nobody lives here," Mama Stella insisted. "This island's been deserted for years. I'm turning around before my tires get caught in the sand."

"Seamus lives in one of these cottages. I've followed him before." Lyman was peering past her. "Look for his red motorcycle."

"You've followed him before, or you've been to his house?" Bella Stella screeched. "We're supposed to search for my Mickey, not some cop who you think has a magical dog."

"I didn't say the dog was magical. I said the dog magically appears and disappears." Lyman hated to be misquoted.

"What's the difference?" Bella fumbled through her purse and found her crocheted cigarette case. "I need a smoke. Where are my matches?" Lyman held the wheel while Mama Stella dug to the bottom of her over-stuffed handbag. "That mook son of mine probably threw them all out." She grabbed the wheel again. "Broke the lighter in the car on purpose too."

"Maybe he doesn't want you to get cancer."

"Yeah, you can get cancer from worrying. About your kids!" Bella shouted. "Smoking calms my nerves, and yelling keeps my lungs clear of cancer germs."

Lyman knew a rebuttal would be futile.

"Look!" Bella pointed.

This time Lyman had the foresight to brace himself before Mama Stella slammed on the brakes. Putting his feet on the dashboard kept his bottom on the seat.

"There's a light on in that house."

"It's gotta be Seamus's place," Lyman said. "Pull over."

Bella took her foot off the brake and coasted to the edge of the narrow road. She rolled the window down and poked her head out, making certain not to drive her tire into the surrounding dunes. She shifted the moon buggy into park, cranked up the window, and cut the engine. Mama appeared ready for action. "I got a .22 in the glove box."

"A gun?" Lyman pressed himself away from her, against the car door. He began to doubt his favorable opinion of the blue-haired woman beside him.

"Whatta you scared of?" Bella opened the glove compartment. A shiny pearl-handled revolver sat atop a pile of maps. "A Mother's Day gift from Mickey."

Lyman slammed the glove box, almost catching Bella's fingers. "Seamus isn't dangerous; we don't need a gun."

"Relax, you old poop." Mama Stella rubbed her unharmed digits. "I didn't say we had to *fire* the gun, just use it to get the copper to fess up what he knows about Mickey."

"No, no guns! I told you, we're just here to spy on Seamus."

"Whatever." Bella shrugged. She opened her car door and stepped out. "Coming? Or are you scared?"

"I'm not afraid of firearms," Lyman insisted. "I once trained with a Marine recon artillery unit while I was writing an article on—"

"Yeah, yeah, you're full of stories. Now hurry up." Bella locked the driver's side and slid the car keys into her pocketbook.

Lyman hoisted himself out of the low-riding Pacer and closed the heavy, curved passenger door harder than necessary.

The moon buggy rocked and the glove compartment latch disengaged, leaving the .22 exposed.

"Follow me," Mama Stella ordered. "This cop better have some answers."

Seamus was dressed and ready to motor when he heard the crunching of sand outside his window. He cut the kitchen light, pressed himself against the wall, and peered through a gap in the mini-blinds. A familiar voice caught Seamus's attention.

"Quit pushing me, Bella," Lyman said, in a stage whisper.

"You're too slow!" Bella retorted, louder than Lyman. "It's going to be sundown soon and I don't like this place. Why did we have to sneak the long way through these scratchy weeds when there's a deck leading to the front door?"

"Because we are *trying* to be surreptitious."

"Whatever the hell that means." She kicked a clump of reeds; sand sprayed on Lyman.

"Hey!"

Seamus stifled a laugh. "Bluebeard," he whispered. "We've got visitors. Ole Lyman Newlin and…" Seamus squinted and focused his eyes. "A talking troll."

"Shut-up! He'll hear us!" Bella scolded.

"You're the one kicking sand."

Seamus tiptoed to the front door and opened it a crack. "Who's there? Fang, here boy! Fang, sic'm!" Seamus stomped his foot and cupped both hands over his mouth. "WOOF, WOOF, WOOF, WOOF! Grrrrr… WOOF, WOOF!"

"He let the dog loose!" Lyman screamed. "Run!"

Seamus's ferocious dog impression accomplished its objective.

Lyman and Bella made a mad dash away from the bungalow, in the opposite direction of the road. The unsure footing caused their stubby legs to buckle and tangle. The dynamic duo fell over one another into a soft dune.

"Get off me you idiot!" Bella punched Lyman in the neck.

"Ow! You didn't have to hit me!" Lyman rubbed his skin.

"I told you we should have brought the gun!"

Seamus howled again and watched the portly peeping Toms scurry out of sight. "Nothing like live comedy, huh Bluebeard?" Seamus rolled his bike out and locked the cottage door behind him. He guided the motorcycle down the walkway to the street where the Pacer was parked. He peeked inside the car. "Well look here."

Seamus opened the passenger door and helped himself to the revolver. *Not three times in one day.* Seamus threw the gun with all his werewolf might. It landed 400 yards away in the ocean. For an encore he released the moon buggy brake and pushed it into a mound of sand.

Seamus cranked his motorcycle.

"He's getting away!" Lyman and Bella exclaimed in unison.

Seamus's keen ears caught the remark. He fastened his helmet and full-throttled the Beemer back towards Highway 99. "But this time you won't follow me!"

By the time the winded twosome returned to their sand-stranded ride, Seamus was no where in sight.

Two hazy figures appeared in the reeds next to Lyman and Bella. *Los padres.* The dynamic duo didn't take notice of the ghostly couple.

"This is all your fault!" Bella panted and punched Lyman in the arm.

"Will you quit hitting me!" Lyman rubbed his sleeve.

Paz walked through Bella.

"Did you feel that?" Bella paused.

"Of course I felt you punch me!"

"Not that." Bella looked around, eyeing the deserted dunes. "A cold burst of air just made my hair stand on end. I hate this island. I wanna leave."

"Me too, but first things first. How are we going to get your car out of the sand?" Lyman surveyed the situation. "Maybe you can put some wood planks under the tires."

"¡*Vieja loca*!" Paz said. "She's a crazy old woman!" Paz waved her hand in front of Bella's face.

Mama Stella screamed, "I felt it again!"

"The wind is blowing. Stop shrieking," Lyman pleaded. "You're gonna give me another heart attack."

Salvador laughed. "*Mala*, you are bad, frightening the old woman."

"She is causing many *problemas*." Paz floated up and sat on the roof of the car.

Salvador joined his wife.

"That Sullivan…" Lyman shook his head.

"I think the wolf was very smart to bark and push the car into sand." Paz smiled.

"Ah, so you are becoming fond of the wolf?" Salvador. smiled "*¿Sí?*"

"*Sí, un poco,*" Paz confessed. "A little bit."

"*Bueno*. I like him too," her husband agreed.

"Do something! If Mickey was here we wouldn't still be stuck," Bella rasped.

"Can you do anything besides nag?" Lyman kicked the tire.

Salvador shook his head. "We cannot let these two follow the wolves."

"Ha! They will be caught in the sand forever." Paz swiped her foot through Lyman's head.

"Hey, I just felt it too, that cold air." Lyman quivered. "It was like a blast of Arctic shooting through my brain."

"I told you!" Bella opened the driver's side door. "I'm getting outa here! Hop in!"

Lyman obeyed.

Bella started the car and put it into reverse. The spinning rear tires dug deeper into the sand dune. She shifted into drive and hit the gas. Her front tires drilled into the white mound.

"*Mira*,"Paz laughed. "*Dos estúpidos.*"

Salvador floated beside the vehicle for a better view of the sinking.

"The old man only cares to write a famous story, and the crazy woman is not going to find her son who was eaten by the wolf," Paz said.

"We must send them on a wild goose hunt," Salvador replied.

Mama Stella gunned the Pacer. Four spinning wheels shot sand in every direction. The loose dune collapsed onto the hood of her car.

"Because of Mickey, *los locos* are interfering with *los lobos*," Paz quipped.

"We will think of a plan." Salvador rubbed his chin.

Paz noticed a dim figure approaching. "Salvador," she whispered and pointed.

"*¿Qué?*" Salvador turned around and saw a dark gray blobby phantom cloud.

"*Es el hijo,*" Paz said. "Mickey!"

"Her son! Where is his light?" Salvador inquired.

"*Malo, él no tiene la luz.*" Paz floated behind her husband. "He is the same dark as his soul."

Mickey walked past *los padres* without giving them a glance.

"*Oscuro, como un diablo,*" Paz said.

"True. No light, like a demon," Salvador marveled.

"I'm sorry, Mama," Mickey blubbered outside the window of the trapped Pacer. The car jerked forward and back. "Mama, it's me, Mickey." He rubbed his hand across the glass. "I'm here."

"She can't see or hear you," Paz answered.

Mickey shoved his misty dim head through the windshield. "Mama!"

"Shhh," Salvador hushed his wife. "Don't speak to him."

"He cannot harm me." Paz glided over to Mickey.

Mickey pulled his head out of the windshield and struck a defensive pose. "What do you want, lady?"

"One minute you are crying like a baby and the next you are rude."

"If you haven't noticed, I'm not that bright," Mickey said. "I got a problem here."

"This *problema* is all your fault," Paz scolded. "Your mami is searching for you, and the reporter is interfering because you shot the werewolf and he ate you." She shook her finger at Mickey. "You did many bad things when you lived."

Mickey sniffled and wiped his nose across his sleeve. "So, I fu—," he caught Paz's glare. "I messed up, and now they won't let me in." Mickey pointed up.

"You cannot pass to the other side with no light," Paz said.

Salvador took his wife by the arm. "*Venga.*"

"*Un momento.*" Paz kept her eyes fixed on Mickey. "You must do something good. Help your mami if you wish to pass over to the light."

The passenger door swung open. "Don't worry, Bella. We can make it to the highway." Lyman walked around and assisted a sobbing Mama Stella out of the car.

"Where is Mickey? What if I never see my son again?" Bella cried. "He's mean and stupid, but he's all I got."

Lyman comforted her. "We'll find him."

"Mickey's got the most beautiful vegetable garden. He can grow green peppers this big!" Bella made a big circle with her hands. "And the sweetest tomatoes."

"I'm sure your son is a wonderful gardener," Lyman assured her.

"Mama," Mickey moaned. "I'm here. Your stupid mook is right next to you."

She walked through him. "I got that chill again, The coldest one yet!" Mama Stella clutched her jacket. "Wish I'd listened to Mickey and bought a cell phone."

Lyman took Bella's arm. "I left mine at the office. There's probably a pay phone near the highway exit ramp. I'll call us a cab."

"Hey you! Don't touch my mama!" Mickey took a swipe at Lyman.

The reporter responded with a shiver. "The breeze is getting colder."

The newly formed dynamic duo walked along the road, arm in arm, into the setting Saturday sun.

"Mama! Come back, Mama!"

"Mickey," Salvador said. "Your mami will be OK."

"But look at me," Mickey whined. "I'm going to the Darkside." Mickey threw himself onto the car hood. "I'm a bad boy!" he wailed and thrashed.

"Hush!" Paz scolded him. "Control yourself!"

"Think. What can you fix from your life?" Salvador asked.

"A big, fat, mean bully!" Mickey screeched.

"Can you change a wrong that you have done?" Salvador continued. "Be a man."

"And keep your mami and the reporter away from Seamus and the other werewolves?" Paz added. She had a personal agenda.

Mickey quieted and scratched his head. "I gotta help my mother and the werewolves? There's more than one?"

"Yes," Paz replied. "And you must help them unless you want to spend eternity with evil sprits like yourself. *Diablos*." She winked at her husband.

"I don't know," Mickey mumbled. He floated in circles. "Maybe, I could…"

"What?" Salvador responded with a glimmer of hope.

"There is one thing, one thing I did that maybe I could sorta fix," Mickey said. He stared off into space with a dazed look on his face.

"What?" Paz prompted.

"But how to make my mama believe I wasn't a total loser?" Mickey seemed to be lost in a deep thought. "OK, you're gonna have to help," Mickey said with sudden enthusiasm.

Los padres gave each other an apprehensive look.

Mickey soared up, above the lamppost. "C'mon," he called. "Follow me!"

Chapter 14

THE DEEP

"Burp!" A brownish sulfury beelzebubble belched its way through a newly burrowed crack in the subway tunnel floor. It floated up through the deep dank darkness with an objective, a destination, an intended victim.

"Burp!" The beelzebubble floated higher. "Burp!" Higher still.

"Burp, burp!" Two quick consecutive burps meant, "The coast is clear; come join the pungent procession."

"Burp!" A larger beelzebubble belched its way through the same earthen crevice. The second smelly brown cloud caught up to the first, combining to create a bigger and even stinkier puff of dread.

The cross-park G train rattled and roared through the passageway. Its violent vibration shook everything in its transitory trail, including a cinderblock-sized chunk of corroded cement. Chunk quivered, jittered, and dislodged from the crumbling wall. The liberated brick landed flat smack atop the beelzebubbles' portal.

"Burp, burp!" the first beelzebubble called, yet again.

Beelzebubble three belched in reply and floated up. Unlike one and two, number three met with strong resistance. Three belched again with all its might, but could not budge the barrier that now blocked its escape.

"Burp! Burp!" foul bubble two called. It was growing

impatient.

Bubble three enlisted bubble four's assistance. "BBUURPP!" their combined belch wasn't blustery enough to dislodge the big brick.

"BURP! BURP!" beelzebubbles one and two commanded in unison. They stopped floating. They waited... and waited... and waited... Beelzebubbles three and four did not appear.

"Burp!" The conjoined beelzebubbles abandoned the trapped others and belched on through the deep darkness.

Together, one and two seeped into a fault in the south tunnel barrier, a structure fracture that led to a forsaken corridor. "Burp!" The brownish beelzebubble floated with putrid programmed purpose towards the projected target. "Burp!"

Claudia set down the book she was reading and glanced at her watch. "It's way past my bedtime, nearly time to wake up, if I were home, safe and sound in my own bed."

"Yes, Miss." Simon hovered beside the cot, watching Claudia's every move like an attentive puppy. "I liked to drink warm milk before sleep."

"Me too." Claudia rubbed her eyes and yawned. "But I'm not going to sleep, even though I am very tired." She adjusted her pillows. "There's a reason why Sevlow bookmarked some of these pages."

Her brain was full of ferocious facts and fallacies, but she wasn't sure how to tell one from the other. Claudia was almost positive werewolves didn't feed on the brains of newborns. She also didn't believe they could morph into other animal shapes, sprout leathery wings, and fly to distant galaxies.

However, one book segment had piqued Claudia's interest more than the rest.

Claudia pulled a paperback from the middle of the pile. A circa 1969 romance novel, IL LUPO APPASSIONATO, told the story of a beautiful, rich Italian Countess who had fallen in love with and married a handsome prince, a prince who transformed into a homicidal werewolf when the moon was full.

Claudia read the bookmarked passage for the second time.

I found Marcello alone in the forest clearing, his velvety fur bathed in the light of the silvery full moon. My heart swelled with rapt fervor. Even in his altered form, my husband was sexy, mysterious, and dangerous, with an element of untamed simmering just below the surface. I hid myself in the shadowy shrubbery as I inched closer.

Prince Marcello the werewolf did not detect my approach until the white, sheer, billowy nightgown I was wearing caught on a jagged branch and tore, exposing my ample breasts.

Marcello was upon me in a flash. I could feel his sharp paw claws against my night-chilled skin, the panting of his hot musky breath on my flushed cheek. In a frenzy, he removed the remaining shreds of my sleeping garment and—

Claudia skipped ahead to the next page.

We lay in the grass, panting passionately from our frolic. Marcello's tail covered my nakedness. I knew what I had to do, to release my beloved husband from the spell that bound him to lunar mayhem. Only I, I who loved him nearly as much as I loved myself, could utter the words that would break the hex and send Marcello to his final resting place, forever.

I held his gaze. "Marcello Antonio di Giovanni Vivaldi," I chanted.

He growled in protest.

"Marcello Antonio di Giovanni Vivaldi," I spoke a second time, although my husband's ebony eyes implored me to stop.

He knew if I, his true love, uttered his given name three times while the werewolf controlled, the gates of Heaven would spring open and his human soul would be eternally released from the lupus curse.

Sweet death awaited my husband. "Marcello Antonio di Giovanni Vivaldi," I spoke for the third and final time.

The reverse enchantment was now complete.

Marcello howled and writhed and moaned in protest, but it was too late. Within a moment my husband's mortal human body lay at my side. Marcello tenderly grasped my petite bejeweled hand, took his last breath, and expired.

As soon as his soul was freed to Heaven, the lifeless carcass that remained turned to dust and scattered upon the night breeze.

My Marcello was no more.

I wept.

Claudia closed the book.

Beelzebubbles floated along in the deep darkness that was the forgotten bowels of New City. "Burp!"

If a beelzebubble had a brain and could ponder, it just might wonder why a city as large and as heavy as New City didn't collapse into the jigsaw of abandoned tunnels below. Surely the weight of trucks, asphalt streets, skyscrapers, and an over-abundance of inhabitants was enough to produce a giant sinkhole?

"Burp!" The brown stinky cloud squeezed between two stone blocks whose mortar had crumbled. Beelzebubbles one and two found themselves in a lighted corridor. But since beelzebubbles don't ponder or have eyes, they did not notice the glowing torches or the young woman seated on a cot holding a book. They also did not hear her gag as they passed through the room.

Beelzebubbles one and two traversed the room and departed the same way they had entered, righting a wrong turn on the journey to their destination. "Burp!"

"Oh my gosh! Simon, is that smell coming from you?" Claudia dropped IL LUPO APPASSIONATO and covered her nose.

"It wasn't me, Miss," Simon said.

"Is there a sewer pipe down here?" Claudia's eyes were tearing.

Simon gave her a perplexed look. He didn't seem to notice the sudden stench.

Claudia let go of her nose and took a quick sniff. "It's gone." She shook off the residual. "That nasty smell came and went. How weird."

"Yes, Miss."

"Simon, I said to call me Claudia."

Simon cast his eyes downward.

"Were you always such a polite little boy?"

"Yes, Miss."

Claudia smiled. "Well, if that stink didn't come from this room." Claudia thought for a moment. "When you left me earlier, Simon, where did you go?"

Simon pointed to the stone wall. "To see my brother."

Claudia hopped off the cot to investigate. "Your brother Benjamin is on the other side of this wall?"

"No, Miss. I must go away to see Benjamin."

Claudia ran her hand along the stones. Her finger slid into a crevice where the mortar had broken free, clear to the other side. Claudia used her fingernail to flick-out another piece of loose cement that surrounded the 12" x 9" stone. "So, you are sure there is no other door, no other exit except the one Sevlow used?"

Simon shook his head. "No door to the place behind the wall either."

"The place behind the wall? Simon, is there more than dirt on the other side of these stones?"

"Yes, Miss. Big rooms. It's dark."

"Big dark rooms? Maybe one of them has an exit to the outside." Claudia sprinted over to the provisions table and grabbed the silverware.

"Are you going to break the wall?" Simon asked, floating up and down.

"Yes, Simon, I'm going to try and remove a few blocks from this wall." She dug a butter knife into the crack and gouged out a long strip of ancient grout. "Wow! It might not continue to be this easy," Claudia said, knocking another chunk to the ground. "But if I can wiggle out at least two stones, I'm pretty sure I'll be able to squeeze myself through to the other side."

"I want to help!" Simon cheered. "I want to chop rocks too!"

"Simon, you're able to toss marbles. I'll bet you can help." Simon clapped.

"You're a special spirit," Claudia observed. "Not all ghosts can move earthly objects." Claudia had read about poltergeists who could move matter. However, she had never met any who possessed the ability, until Simon. *Los padres* weren't able to rearrange items around the house. *Thank goodness.*

"Look!" Simon tossed his marble bag across the room. It landed against the wall with a THUNK!

Claudia marveled. "You could haunt the heck out of a house!"

For an encore, he pushed the werewolf books to the floor and yanked the covers from the cot. Simon floated over to the food table and eyed the olive oil bottle.

"Hey, come back over here," Claudia called. "Don't even think about it!"

Simon obeyed and floated in reverse. He hovered at her side, sporting a huge mischievous grin. Claudia handed him a fork. Simon could hold the silver utensil in his little grey hand. He drifted to the wall and tapped the prongs against a vein of mortar. A large hunk fell to the ground.

"Amazing!" Claudia exclaimed.

Simon giggled with delight.

Claudia took the fork from Simon's grip. "Too bad forks can't breeze through stone like ghosts." She contemplated for a moment. "Simon, I need you to glide over to the other side of the wall and see if you can find something hard and sharp in the big room, a piece of metal, a jagged rock, a pointy stick." She caught herself before saying, *but don't hurt yourself.*

Simon nodded.

"Chip away at the filling between these two blocks." Claudia traced the target area with her knife. "If I work one side and you work the other we'll break through to the dark room much faster."

"Yes, Miss Claudia." Simon disappeared.

An instant later Claudia heard tapping. "Good boy!"

The beelzebubbles made a left turn at the alligator in the sewer and ascended through the manhole cover outlet. 1 City Avenue loomed ahead of them.

The nefarious beelzebubbles had arrived at their destination.

"Burp!" They belched across the deserted street, between the iron fence posts, past the security guard, over the manicured lawn, and up the freshly painted steps of New City's most famous country house. "Burp!" The beelzebubble made their misty way along the wrap-around porch, and under the front door of Tracie Mansion.

Mayor Fink and his faithful friend, Liberace, slept in the massive master bedroom at the end of the second floor hall.

Their happy Dreamland travels were about to be interrupted.

His Honor was jolted out of his sleep by the arrival of the noxious beelzebubbles. "Uuugh! What the?" Mayor Fink sat up and shook his spotted bed buddy awake. "Liberace, go, out, bye-bye!"

The drowsy dog thumped his tail, but didn't budge from his warm spot at the foot of the comforter.

"Shoo, doggie door, potty!" His Honor swiped his foot along the bottom of the top sheet until Liberace was coaxed off the bed. Mayor Fink turned on his night table light and pointed to the bedroom door. He planted his feet on the carpeted floor and gave the command. "Out!"

Liberace slinked towards the exit, eyes and tail downcast.

"I'm sorry if your feelings are hurt," His Honor apologized to the innocent hound. "No more table scraps for you!"

The dog resisted at the threshold.

His Honor closed the door on Liberace's behind, sliding him the final few inches through the door and into the hall. He slammed the bedroom door.

"It still stinks in here."

Before Mayor Fink had the chance to open a window, the two beelzebubbles separated and struck, entering His Honor's body through separate orifices.

The Mayor gasped and shook and dropped onto his knees with a THUD.

Liberace hadn't left the hallway.

The mayor moaned.

"Woof!" Liberace scratched at the shut door.

Mayor Fink clutched his throat and struggled for breath. His eyes rolled back in their sockets. Drool spilled from the side of his mouth. He fell forward onto the rug, unconscious.

Liberace whimpered and dug, pushed and cried until the door opened. He bounded in, to the rescue. Liberace licked his master's face.

The mayor stirred.

Sniff, sniff, sniff, sniff. Liberace cocked his head.

Mayor Fink sat up and scanned the room, blinking, focusing, as if using an unfamiliar set of eyes.

Liberace took a step back and growled, "Rrrrrrr!"

His Honor's pupils were fully dilated; his skin had lost its tanning booth glow. Without warning the imposter grabbed the hound by the collar.

Liberace yelped and snapped; his eyetooth tore a strip of skin on the fiend's borrowed wrist.

The intruder released his grip.

Liberace scooted away, fangs exposed. "Grrrr."

Fake Fink made a menacing face, like the demon he was. "Yes, little doggie, you are correct. I am not your beloved master. I am a visitor from The Deep, and I've come to destroy New City. Ha-ha-ha!"

Chapter 15

STORMY WEATHER

Alex stood at his hotel room window staring at the frozen city below. Early April and Bean Town was blanketed in winter white. A cold, dry, Canadian front moved south and intermingled with a warm, moist air mass trekking north from the Gulf of Mexico. Their merger caused decreased atmospheric pressure and a sizable barometric flux. In other words, enough snow had fallen to cancel an entire weekend Bomber vs. Red Coat rivalry series. But Alex wasn't concerned about stormy weather or postponed baseball games; he was worried about Claudia. She hadn't answered any of his calls. Alex sent his sister another text message: WHERE R U? He stared at the cell phone screen waiting for a reply that never arrived.

TJ darted out of his lair. "What's that annoying sound?" he shouted, rummaging through heaps of wolf den debris. "I can't finish a thought without being interrupted by, BEEP BEEP BEEP!" He tossed both sofa cushions onto the floor. "Supersonic senses have a downside."

"I don't hear anything," Dragon replied. A wadded tissue protruded from each of his ears.

"Man, you're not right!" TJ threw a box of Sneeze Puffs in his friend's direction.

Dragon deflected the carton with his elbow. It ricocheted off a dusty lampshade and smacked Sevlow in the chest as he entered the room.

"He did it!" Dragon and TJ pointed at one another.

Sevlow inquired, "Have you checked the smoke alarm battery?"

"Yeah, Fire Marshall Bill. That's your job." TJ charged, swiping a cotton puff from Dragon's ear. "Now hear this: find a 9 volt before I go beeping nuts and knock the mu-shu outta you."

Dragon lifted his butt cheek and released a trumpet of air. "Mu-shu served."

"Oh yeah," TJ swallowed a whopping gulp of air and spoke through a forced belch. "EEAATT TTHHIISS!"

Sevlow did not acknowledge the brotherly bathroom banter.

Mighty Mouse slid out from under the ratty ottoman holding Claudia's purse. "It's coming from in here." He handed Sevlow the red leather handbag.

Sevlow unzipped the pocketbook and removed Claudia's flashing cell phone. He handed it to Dragon. "Check the messages."

Dragon examined the phone and punched a series of buttons on the keypad. "She has three unread text messages, all from the same number: *Good ride? ... Call me...* And, *Where R U?*" Dragon pressed another series of keys. "There are two new voicemail messages from the same number as the texts."

Alex's voice played through the tiny speaker. "Hey, Claudia. Hope you had a fun ride with Pirate. The plane's about to take off and the captain says storms are in the forecast. Maybe the weatherman's wrong. I'm really looking forward to this series. Anyway, gimme a call later. We should be at the hotel by two. Love ya."

"Ew! He loves her!" Mighty Mouse jeered.

Dragon hit the NEXT button.

"Claudia, haven't heard back from you. Sent a text message too. Didn't think you went anywhere without your phone. The team just had a meeting. It's a blizzard here. Sunday's double-header been postponed too, and the airports are closed. Guess there are worse places to be stranded on a Saturday night. Maybe I can find an open titty bar? Ha-ha, just kidding. The storm's headed south, towards New City. Let me know you're alright. Love ya."

Dragon was still holding the phone when it began to play the William Tell Overture. "Answer it?" he asked. "What if her brother's calling again?"

"Sure, Inspector Gadget, answer it." TJ threw himself onto the cushionless sofa. "Tell Bomber boy to quit calling; his sister is safe and sound, locked away."

Sevlow took the phone from Dragon's hand. "Where's Seamus?"

"He brought a radio to the sarge," Dragon replied.

"Good," Sevlow nodded. "Finish preparing. I need to pay Ms. Peña a visit before Seamus returns."

Alex sat in the back of a green and white Metro Cab.

"Sis, me again. I just phoned the Tacoma and Freddy said he hasn't seen you since this morning when you left for the stables. He even went upstairs and banged on the apartment door. You don't go anywhere after riding without a shower and ten outfit changes. I'm worried." Alex paused to prevent his voice from cracking. He couldn't imagine what he'd do if anything ever happened to Claudia. Alex pushed the thought from his mind. "Bean Town's on transit lock down, but I found a cabbie who'll drive me to New City. It's costing your entire month's allowance. Don't be upset—you're worth it." Alex forced a nervous laugh. "Hey, call me. Whenever you get in. From the looks of these roads, I probably won't be home before dawn. Love ya." Alex set his phone down on the seat beside him. "Mami, Papi…" He leaned his forehead against the frigid window. "Wherever you are, please keep Claudia safe."

"We did it!" Claudia shouted, after dislodging the last of the two passage stones from the tomb wall. "Can't believe we actually broke through to the other side! In record time! If there is a record for mortar-chipping!"

Simon shot out of the open hole. "I helped, Miss Claudia!"

"Yes, you did, Simon! I could not have done this without you." Claudia tried to give the little ghost a big hug. Her arms met with a current of cold air. She had to settle for kudos. "We make a great team!"

Simon clapped. "Yeah!"

152

Claudia joined in giving a round of applause. She caught sight of her dirty fingers and shrugged. "Who needs manicured nails?" Claudia picked off the last flake of red polish from her pinky.

There was a loud BOOM of thunder.

"If I can hear a storm brewing. Wonder if it's thunder-snow? This passageway must lead to civilization." She wedged her head through the wall outlet, looked around, and then pulled it back inside the room. "Wow, it's dark and cold out there. Probably filthy too." Claudia brushed a cobweb from her hair, put on her red riding jacket, and canvassed the provisions Sevlow had brought.

"Can we go?" Simon floated in and out of the opening.

"I need a minute. I should bring some supplies, just in case." Claudia packed the first-aid kit, some bottled waters, the flashlight, and IL LUPO APPASSIONATO into the empty book sack. Her stomach growled. "Guess I worked up an appetite." Claudia grabbed a loaf of bread from the basket and took a bite. "I could eat this whole thing," she said between chews. "But then we'd have to knock out another stone." Claudia swallowed and shoved the remainder of the loaf into her bag. She unhooked a lantern from the wall and hesitated for a second. She walked back over to the supply table and added the roll of toilet paper to her sack. "OK, think we're ready."

Simon drifted into the darkness.

Claudia passed the supply satchel through the hole. "I'm next." She pulled her hands into her sleeves before placing two fists on the mystery ground and hoisting the remainder of her body out of the opening. Claudia didn't relish the thought of her skin touching whatever comprised the dark moist ground.

"Want to meet my brother?" Simon asked. He pointed to the right.

Claudia wasn't looking at him as she attempted to sweep a clump of soggy muck from her jacket cuff. It smeared across her red cashmere sleeve. "Let's visit your brother some other time," she replied, not wanting to disappoint him. "Right now I have to find my friend, Seamus. He needs help." Claudia looped her arms into the handles of the burlap satchel so it wore like a backpack. She held up the glowing lantern. "We're in some sort of underground tunnel. There's a cold draft coming from…" Claudia licked her finger and held it up. It was something she learned from her brother. Before getting into his batting stance, Alex would judge the direction of the wind and which way it would be pulling the ball. He could just as easily have looked at the outfield flags to judge the wind direction, but finger-licking was one of his many superstition rituals. "A breeze is coming from the left," Claudia surmised. "We should walk that way."

"Yes, Miss Claudia." Simon glided into the cool current of air.

There was another clap of thunder. Claudia buttoned her soiled red riding coat. "Sounds like we're in for some very stormy weather."

Once upon a time the New City Transportation Authority collected change from drivers exiting the Eastside Expressway onto Round Island.

Exact coins and tokens, veer to the right, toss your money in to the mechanical basket, and wait for the automated arm to rise. Need change or a receipt? Keep left.

Lyman and Mama Stella sat shivering and huddled in the last intact abandoned tollbooth. Two freezing peas in a porous pod.

The North wind hooted and howled. Icy pellets slapped against the stall's graffiti-covered panels. Sleet and snow trickled down cracks in the threadbare roof.

It was a night neither fit for man nor beast.

"I'm going to die!" Bella cried. "I'm going to freeze to death in this quarter-taker's coffin and never see my son Mickey again!"

"There, there." Lyman patted her shoulder and snuggled closer.

Bella didn't resist.

Lyman slipped his arm through hers.

She didn't object when he grasped her hand.

He treated it as an open invitation. Lyman inched even nearer and pressed his 12-hour stubble cheek against Bella's jowly face, puckered his pasty lips, closed his wistful eyes, and leaned into Mama Stella's solid right hook.

"OW!"

"Try smooching on me again, you old poop, and I'll give you stormy weather!"

Lyman scooted to the far side of the leaky booth.

Mama Stella mumbled under her breath. *Bless me father for I wanna sin. It's been twenty-four years, eleven months, and five days since my last kiss.*

KNOCK! KNOCK!

Sevlow banged upon the tomb door. "Miss Peña, it's Sevlow. I am about to enter the chamber." There was no reply. Sevlow was not alarmed by the silence. Claudia had slept soundly through the supply delivery. "Miss Peña?"

BEEP! BEEP! Alex's latest message had triggered the call signal.

Sevlow unlocked the massive door. It opened with a loud CREAK. He crossed the threshold and strode down the long hall. "Miss Peña," he repeated in a gentle tone. "Are you awake?" His voice echoed down the corridor.

Sevlow entered the illuminated sleeping quarters. He found the cot and the room unoccupied. Sevlow spotted the dislodged stones and escape hole.

"Ah, Miss Peña?" Sevlow set the BEEPing phone on the supply table. He took a mental inventory of supplies, and then sorted through the pile of werewolf books. Sevlow observed which one was missing. He shook his head. "Miss Peña," he said aloud. "You have made a decision, now fate must determine your future."

There was another booming clap of thunder.

"I can no longer protect you from the storm you may soon weather."

Chapter 16

MONSTER MASH

Paz and Salvador followed Mickey to a vegetable garden in the far corner of his mother's overgrown backyard. Thirty yards of makeshift chicken wire fencing enclosed the perimeter of the waterlogged plot. A white weathered clapboard shed stood at the front of the planted area. A rake and shovel leaned against a pitted wheelbarrow that blocked the shed's entrance. Snow accumulated along the building's rusted gutters and muddy water froze atop its crumbling foundation. Mickey came to an abrupt halt at the gate to the enclosure.

"What?" Paz plowed into his massive murky derrière. "¿Qué pasa?"

"You go first," Mickey mumbled with trepidation in his voice. "What if they're all waiting for me?"

"¿Quién? Who is waiting for you?" Paz scanned the area. It was deserted.

"What is the problem?" Salvador asked. "What do you want to show us?"

Mickey didn't have a chance to respond.

"There he is!" announced an entity.

"Look, the big fat bastard is dead!" yelled another from beyond.

"Get him!" screamed a third.

"I'm outa here!" Mickey attempted to flee, but it was too late. The four remains of his hit man past surrounded him. They weren't in high spirits.

"¡Díos mío!" Paz and Salvador exclaimed. They soared clear of the ambush and watched events unfold from atop the tree branches.

"Good to see you're dead. The day was bound to come and I'm glad it was sooner rather than later you son of a—"

An angry woman holding her crudely severed head was interrupted by a tall thin man with a pick ax protruding from his skull. Brains and gore still oozed from the mortal hack wound. "What goes around comes around. How does it feel to be in limbo?"

A blood-spattered armless carcass interjected. "From the looks of your dimness, you've earned a one-way ticket to the Darkside. Hope you roast for an eternity!"

A charred cadaver groaned in agreement.

Mickey clenched his fists and struck a defensive pose. "Get away from me or I'll—" His threat was dismissed before it was complete.

"Otherwise you'll do what?" challenged the talking head. "Or you'll murder us?" She lifted up her scowling face so it was nose-to-nose with Mickey. "Was decapitation my husband's idea or yours? Was kidnapping and killing a mother of three worth a lousy five-grand? Did he think it would keep me from nagging? Nag, nag, nag, nag…"

"Stop it!" Mickey covered his ears.

158

"Nag, nag, nag, nag! Bet you don't even know my name!"

"Or mine," pick-axed cranium continued.

"Or mine," armless torso guy chimed.

"Mmmm," burnt body moaned.

"Nag, nag, nag, nag!"

"Shut up!" Mickey yelled. "I know who you are—you're all vegetables." Mickey pointed to each of the gruesome ghosts, beginning with the headless accuser, and ending with cinder-fella. "Tomatoes, peppers, zucchini, and rutabaga. Mix yous all together and whadaya get?"

The four looked to one another for the answer.

Tomatoes responded for the group. "A salad?"

"Monster mash! Get it? Mix rotting stiffs all together. Monster mash?" Mickey let out a hearty chuckle.

The salad four were on Mickey in an instant, like they were a brigade of E. Coli, and he was a slice of room-temperature roast beef, post green and shimmery.

Mickey swatted and swung, but the quartet kept up the onslaught of ghastly groaning and groping. Mickey bounced from one cadaver to another like a pinball on TILT. Tomatoes added in-your-face personal insults to the physical assault.

"Lardo, brainless, despicable, scum!" she jeered.

Los padres floated down from their perch above.

"*¡Basta ya!*" Paz shouted. "Enough!"

The repugnant pandemonium paused.

"Who are you two?" Peppers asked. "You friends of this creep?"

The angry bunch averted their attention away from Mickey.

Salvador positioned himself between his wife and the frenzied foursome. "My wife and I are here to see if we can help you. Mickey said—"

Tomatoes interrupted. "I wouldn't believe anything he says," she pointed at Mickey. "He told me his car broke down and he needed to use my telephone. I let him into the house and now look at me!"

"Yeah," Peppers said. "He tricked us, killed us, buried us, and planted on us. And worst of all, Mickey and his mother ate vegetables grown in our guts!"

Paz covered her mouth and gagged.

"Imagine how we feel?" Zucchini cried. "I thought he was the friend of a friend, offering me a ride into town and now his mother makes me into bread! There ain't a whole lotta trust between the four of us and Mickey the murderer for hire."

"Yeah!" came the crowd consensus.

"What if Mickey could help you?" Salvador asked in a calming voice. "Help you leave limbo. Could you forgive Mickey, just enough to save him from the Darkside?"

"Never!" Tomatoes shouted.

"Rrrrr!" Rutabaga roared.

"Zero chance of that!" scoffed zucchini.

"Leave limbo?" Peppers pondered. "What's your plan?"

Salvador smiled. "You wait in limbo because murdered

spirits refuse to move on until the truth is told. The ones you love do not know that you are dead. They believe you are still missing and continue searching and hoping for your safe return. Yes?"

"Not my husband!" Tomatoes interjected.

"But perhaps your children," Salvador continued. "Your daughters and sons, they would like to put their mami's body to rest in a proper cemetery? And say goodbye."

"My children!" Tomatoes let out a woeful sob. "They have no idea I'm dead. Their no good father told them I moved to Cincinnati." She wiped her teary face on the hem of her skirt. "I want my homicidal husband arrested and convicted!"

"Yeah," piped in Peppers. "If you want us to forgive Mickey for what he did to us, forgive him a teeny-tiny bit, then we want our families to know we've been murdered and buried in a vegetable garden, and we also want the slimes who contracted our killings to be ratted out and arrested too."

"I ain't no stool pigeon," Mickey snapped. "Yous can all go to—"

Paz shook her finger in Mickey's face. "No, *Malo*, you can go to *los diablos. Es su decisón*, your choice. *¡Mírelo!* Look at yourself!"

Mickey held out his hands. His faint light was fading into complete obscurity. He panicked. "Ok, I'll talk! Don't let me go to the Darkside! I'll tell. I'll tell everything I know! I'll make my mama proud!"

"I don't trust him," Tomatoes scoffed. "What assurance do we have? He's dead, and so are you two."

161

"*No te preocupe*," Paz responded with an accompanying hand wave.

"Yes, do not worry," Salvador agreed.

"Don't worry?" protested peppers. "We're all dead. Who's gonna tell our story and help release our spirits?"

"We will speak to our daughter," Salvador took Paz by the arm.

"She dearly departed or living?" Peppers asked.

"Alive. Claudia is a clairvoyant," Salvador said. "She will assist us. My wife and I must go. Remain here."

"Me too?" Mickey, asked scanning his hostile company. "Stay here? With them?"

"*Sí*," Paz instructed. "And behave yourself, *Malo*."

Before Mickey could protest, *los padres* disappeared.

Sunrise was shielded by a curtain of white.

Liberace scurried into the kitchen behind plaid pajama-wearing fake Fink. The faithful canine frantically nipped at the imposter's bare heels and growled, "GRRRRRR!"

"Go ahead, hound. Bite your master's flesh. Leave tears and gashes. I'll discard this borrowed battered body soon enough!" The beelzebubble laughed. "After we unplug the portal and set off the celebration explosives, Deep havoc will rock the city. Crime rates will soar, tourists will stay away, and for an encore I'll lay off sanitation workers and litter will pile up in the panicked streets!"

Liberace tilted his head towards the door. Someone else was coming. Sniff, sniff, sniff. It smelled like breakfast lady. He barked a warning. "WOOF, WOOF, WOOF!"

Fake Fink slipped behind the pantry door.

Mrs. Cooke the pastry chef and meals coordinator entered the room still sporting her snowy woolen winter coat, hat, and gloves. Her coffee-colored skin contrasted the dusting of rapidly melting flakes. "My goodness, what is that smell!" She gagged and began checking cabinets and drawers for the odor's origin. "Something has rotted or spoiled! Where is that stink coming from? It will spoil Mayor Fink's breakfast." Mrs. Cooke noticed Liberace sitting beneath the utility sink beside the pantry.

He looked up at her with his big brown eyes and thumped his tail.

"You smelly old hound!" she scolded. "Snow or no snow, take your spotted self out that doggie door and go potty!" She gave him a nudge with the toes of her green galoshes. "Now get, and don't come back until you get rid of whatever ain't agreeing with that tummy of yours!"

While her back was turned, fake Fink slithered out of the pantry and into the adjacent foyer.

The hound was in pursuit.

The imposter crouched behind a life-size statue of Fiorello LaGuardia and made two quick phone calls.

"... the parade fireworks, IMMEDIATLY or sooner, delivered to..."

Liberace crouched in the kitchen doorway, keeping his phony master within sight.

The mayor hung up and dialed again. "Mayor Fink here....This is an executive directive... I want the G and M subways..."

"Grrrrrr! WOOF! WOOF!"

Mrs. Cooke grabbed Liberace by the collar and yanked. "Don't you growl and bark at me, mister, lest you've forgotten who fills that kibble bowl." She dragged him back into the kitchen, along the checkered tile, and over to the doggie door. "Go outside before I banish you from my kitchen, forever!"

A noxious brown beelzebubble floated in from the foyer and headed towards Mrs. Cooke. Liberace's dog senses saw it and sounded another warning at his food human, "WOOF, WOOF, AWOOO!"

It was too late. Mrs. Cooke took a beelzebubble to the nostril and was down for the count, twitching and jerking on the cold kitchen floor.

Liberace tried to lick her nose free of the intruder. He would have extracted it too, had counterfeit His Honor not snatched the hound up by the scruff of the neck and tossed him through an opened back door. Liberace landed with a THUD SKID on the icy porch.

Liberace whimpered and howled, but managed to regain his footing and scurry back to the kitchen door. He threw his weight against the bottom panel. A body blow usually dislodged the rusty door catch. Not this time. It was bolted, and so was the doggie flap. Liberace ran around the porch to the breakfast area window. He stood on his hind legs, pressed his wet nose against the frigid glass, and perked his floppy ears. He heard familiar voices chanting in unison.

"One, two, three, four, grab a gizmo and out the door. Five, six, seven, eight, we all crawl down the subway grate. Nine, ten, eleven, twelve, to open the portal we'll dig and delve."

Liberace didn't understand a word of the rhyme, but he did understand when the front door opened and his housemates: cook, gardener, maid, butler, and chauffeur marched zombie-like behind fake Fink, across the white snowy lawn, toward the deserted street. Each was carrying a digging tool: spade, shovel, hoe, trowel, and gravy ladle.

They were going bye-bye without him.

Liberace's primal hound tracking instincts kicked in. He skulked amid the snowdrift shadows, trailing his quarry. Sniff, sniff, sniff.

Fake Fink led the zombie quartet across City Avenue to the subway grate. Fink lifted the metal trap. One-by-one the mayor and his staff descended the grimy emergency ladder to the tunnel below.

165

Liberace bounded from the bushes and raced into the middle of the road. He was too late. The grate had been shut. "WOOF, WOOF!" *Sniff, sniff, sniff.*

They were getting away.

There was a loud HONK. Liberace panicked. He looked to this left, then to his right. Directly in front of him, a KaBoom Celebration delivery truck had been speeding and was now skidding with its brakes jammed-on, through the snow and ice, straight towards Liberace. WHACK! The corner of the bumper caught the spotted hound square in the ribcage and sent him sailing sideways through the air. Liberace landed with a CRACK and a THUMP in the gutter.

The driver rushed from his vehicle. He crouched beside the inert canine and gave him a gentle jostle and push.

Liberace didn't respond.

Liberace stood in a field of green grass and ruby red fire hydrants. There was a basket of squeaky toys and rawhide chews, and a soft pile of something that smelled a lot like rotting fish. Liberace threw himself onto the rancid mound and rolled.

He was in heaven.

"Ah gee. Poor fella," the uniformed deliveryman said through a genuine tear. He checked his watch and looked up and down the street. The coast was clear. "Call me a monster, but I don't got time for this. The mayor wants his firecrackers dropped off in the park ASAP and the snow ain't stopping soon." The harried driver pulled the prone pooch by its tail to the subway grate, lifted the metal corner, and mashed Liberace through the opening. "Sorry, little fella. Don't want you squished here on the avenue, and I ain't got time for a funeral."

Five feet later, Liberace landed with a squishy PLOP.

Liberace grabbed a rubber shoe from the toy basket and returned to the stinky pile to wriggle and chew. *SQUEEKY, SQUEEKY, SQUEEKY…* A faint but familiar voice summoned Liberace from his eternal reverie. He paused to listen.

"Help! Liberace!"

The happy hound dropped the shoe and cocked his head.

"Here boy!"

An open door appeared in the middle of the grassy field.

Liberace set off to investigate. Sniff, sniff, sniff.

"Help me!"

The voice seemed to be coming from beyond the open door.

Liberace peeked inside the crack. On the other side of the door was a black and white spotted hound, lying motionless atop a muddy mound.

Liberace retreated with a start.

"Come, boy, come! Please."

The woeful plea lured the curious dog back to the open door.

"Liberace!"

Liberace glanced back at the lush field of perpetual paradise. Sniff, sniff, sniff. The loyal pooch knew what he had to do.

Liberace felt pain where none had existed a moment earlier. He whimpered and opened his eyes; just enough to see that he was no longer lying in the green, green grass of his new home. There was no turning back. Heaven's door had already disappeared.

Chapter 17

CH, CH, CHANGES

Sergeant Gaffney paced from one end of his office to the other. A sleek 2-way radio protruded from his left breast pocket. Between speech edits and antacid-munching he checked to make certain the walkie-talkie was still where he'd put it, and on receive broadcast mode. Sarge didn't want to take a chance that he'd miss the call or get slowed down by his ulcer. Sergeant Gaffney was practicing for ready. He held his fist to his ear, dialed the air, and rehearsed his impending telephone conversation.

"This is Sergeant Gaffney from the 20th precinct. I have an urgent message for Mayor Fink." He paused, pretending His Honor's secretary was transferring the call. "Sir, Sergeant Gaffney, 20th precinct … Yes, we've met… Thank you. Well, you're doing a fine job too. Your Honor, I am calling because I have a vital intelligence update. The inclement weather has caused a grave security glitch in the Police department's top-secret subterraneous anti-terror bunker…. Well, it's *that* secret… The subway will need to be diverted from the tunnels beneath Midtown Gardens Park for approximately an hour, until the malfunction has been corrected…. Yes, I will take charge of the operation... Of course, I'll inform you as soon as it is safe to run the trains again…. You're very welcome."

Sarge hung up his fist. He thought for a few moments then returned to his draft to make changes. He crossed out "inclement" and inserted "bad".

169

Across the park, Sevlow and his band of merry men gathered in the wolves' den, preparing for their impending dawn departure.

Dragon threw Seamus a new long-sleeved black t-shirt and a pair of camouflage pants. "Uniform... Don't worry—they're clean."

"So, explain to me again about these beelzebubbles," Seamus asked. He pulled off his sweatshirt. "I don't get it. Our mission is to sniff out smelly invisible demons?"

"I hear and I forget. I see and I remember. I do and I comprehend," Dragon replied while putting on his gear.

"Zen werewolf speaks the truth," TJ said. "This whole hounds of the gods business is something you've gotta see and do to really understand."

Seamus tucked in his shirt. The uniform fit. It felt comforting to look, feel, and smell like part of a team.

"Good and evil will always exist," Sevlow said. "However, it is our responsibility to ensure that the proportions remain imbalanced."

"Imbalanced? The hounds of the gods are sent to make sure there's still more good than evil in the world?" Seamus figured that was the pursuit of the hounds.

"Yes," Sevlow said. "Throughout the centuries, the gods' hounds have been diligent and effective watch dogs."

"We're winning," TJ bragged. "Despite global warming, Middle East politics, and the heartbreak of psoriasis."

Sevlow shook his head and broke a brief smile. "Evil reveals itself in many forms, and although beelzebubbles are not as powerful as some malevolent manifestations, they are one of the most devious."

"Weak and wily," Seamus surmised. He was trying to determine what they were up against.

"Wily, but certainly not weak. Not at all," Sevlow cautioned. "If the werewolf is aware and prepared, the beelzebubbles shouldn't pose too much of a physical threat."

"Like annoying flies at a picnic," TJ. explained "Unless the flies buzzing around my ears." TJ shook his head. "That sound will drive me to turn."

"When anger rises, think of the consequences," Dragon offered his wisdom.

"Consequences, schmonsequences, as long as I'm rich," TJ retorted in his best Daffy Duck.

"However, to an unsuspecting werewolf, even one beelzebubble might prove lethal," Sevlow warned. "Mental paralysis and hostage-taking is their forte."

"Similar to an army of *allomerus decemarticulatus*," TJ said. "Never heard of it?"

"Huh?" Seamus replied. "Sounds Greek to me."

"Animal Planet," Mighty Mouse answered. "We watch lots of TV."

"I've noticed." Seamus didn't own a television.

171

"Amazonian ants," TJ said. "Immobilize prey and haul it back to the lair. Beelzebubbles can do the same to a werewolf. Don't let them into your head or you'll wake up rigid down in The Deep, or your thoughts will, anyway."

Seamus was confused. "Literally, inside your head?"

"Exactly. Up your nose, through your ears."

"Up your butt!" Mighty Mouse shouted.

"Wherever they can get in," Dragon cautioned "The little devils will seep into your skull and conquer your thoughts."

TJ's tone became more serious. "They'll find the secrets, bad memories, nightmares, stuff that you've shoved into the dark corners of your brain."

Seamus was used to fighting unpleasant recollections.

"They can paralyze you with your own fear and anger," Dragon said. "We'll help one another stay focused on the external, but we'll also need to keep our own minds occupied. Think of a mantra, one that creates a positive visual."

Seamus thought about breakfast with Claudia. A very appealing visual came to mind, sending a warm rush through his body. He shook it off the sensation. "I got one."

"Right. Keep it PG," TJ teased. "You had no idea Sevlow and me were near during breakfast, because your psyche was NC-17."

Seamus cracked a sheepish grin.

"They work in teams," TJ continued. "Just like us, so we stay together."

"The cautious seldom err," Dragon said reminded as he laced his boots.

"Beelzebubbles like to enlist the aide of humans," Sevlow added. "Either as facilitators or followers. One beelzebubbles can commandeer a human—control words, thoughts, and actions. A single beelzebubble can also stun a small group of humans into slow mindless passive submission."

"Like presidential candidates and TV evangelists," Seamus quipped.

"You're gonna fit right in," TJ laughed. "Exactly."

"In other words, two beelzebubbles are capable of creating an evil dictator and an army of sorta like, zombie followers," Seamus confirmed. He was beginning to understand what they were up against.

"Precisely," Sevlow said. "I received word that the beelzebubbles have established a portal from The Deep, somewhere in the tunnels beneath Midtown Gardens Park. By now they should be close enough for us to detect. It's our mission to locate the outlet and seal it before they can escape and wreck havoc."

"What if they've already broken through?" Seamus asked. "What if they're floating around the city?"

"We round them up," Dragon replied. "And force them back down to the Deep before they can complete their mission."

"How?" Seamus felt like he was way behind the werewolf learning curve. "And how do we seal the beelzebubble portal?"

"We'll continue this information session along the way." Sevlow checked his watch. "Sergeant Gaffney is waiting for our call." He slid a 2-way radio and a GPS into the utility pocket of his black and grey camouflage pants. Sevlow pressed the base of the lighted wall sconce. A section of the wolf den partition slid open, revealing a subterraneous corridor.

Seamus's eyes grew wide. "A secret passageway?"

"The Cock of the Flock has an illustrious history," Sevlow replied with an affirming grin. "The building suits our many clandestine needs."

Claudia walked with the lantern out in front of her. She stopped at a fork in the tunnels trying to decide whether to go left or right.

Simon hovered above her head.

"I don't hear the storm anymore." Claudia observed. "I wonder if that means we've been walking away from an exit that'll lead us out of here."

"Yes, Miss Claudia," Simon said.

"Simon, what do you mean by 'yes'? Are you saying 'yes' we've passed the exit or 'yes' you're also wondering if we're going the right way?" Claudia shivered. "It's freezing down here."

Simon didn't respond. His attention appeared to be elsewhere. Someone was coming.

"It's been hours since we left the tomb and we're still lost; my feet hurt and everything down here is smelly and gross. Bet if I blew my nose, soot would come out." Claudia let out an impatient groan and kicked a wad of sticky muck from her scuffed riding boot. Residue splashed onto her beige riding britches. "Oh! Why did I bother?"

"Do you want to go back to the room, Miss?"

"No, I'll be OK." She took a deep breath. "We'll find a way out of here." Claudia recited a mental eeney-meeny-miney-moe. "Let's go left."

"Hear that, Miss Claudia?" Simon pointed right. "Voices."

"Voices?" Claudia listened for a moment. "I don't hear anything."

"My brother, Benjamin. He's singing a song." Simon darted up and down impatiently. "Let's go see him."

"Your brother? Singing?" Claudia flashed her light. The right side of the tunnel was deserted. "Are you sure? An old person could break a hip walking through these nasty lumpy bumpy tunnels. What would your brother be doing underground?"

Simon disappeared.

"Simon?" Claudia's mood shifted from aggravated to anxious. "Simon, please come back. I didn't mean that you should go off and find the answer to my question…I'm sorry that I'm so grumpy. I need to find a clean bathroom. Simon!" She waited. There was no reply. "Ahhh!" Claudia removed her satchel backpack and pulled out the toilet paper. She braced herself against the corridor wall and dimmed the lantern."This is so disgusting!" Claudia yelled into the abyss. "One minute I'm riding Pirate, and the next relieving myself in a tunnel. Mami! Papi! *¡Ayúdeme!*"

It was Sunday, just after sunrise. Lyman and Bella sat huddled together beneath an itchy wool blanket in the back of a New City highway patrol car. Heat blasted from the vents in the vehicle dashboard.

"You two warming up back there?" the officer behind the wheel asked. "Sure you don't want any of my coffee? It's nice and hot, and a vente." He held up a colossal cardboard cup. "Mochaccino."

"No, thanks," Lyman said. "You've done enough to help out. We appreciate you picking us up."

"He pulled off the expressway to take a leak," Bella growled under her breath. "It was an accident he found us inside the toll booth he was pissing on."

"Shhh." Lyman nudged her in the ribs.

"I can drop you at any of the exits along the expressway. Where you headed?"

"Home!" Bella snapped. "I want to go home."

"If you take us as far as the 12th Street loop, we can walk back to the newspaper and pick up my car." Lyman yawned. "It's been a very long night."

"Sure thing. How about this April snow? Crazy, huh?" The police radio crackled and hissed. The officer adjusted its broadcast frequency.

A woman's voice transmitted through. "10-58 in progress."

"A 10-58?" Lyman repeated. "I'm curious; who gave the orders?"

"Mayor's orders." The officer checked his watch. "Came over about twenty minutes ago."

"What's a 10-58?" Bella asked. "Why'd she talk in code?"

"Protocol. Security-related," Lyman replied in affected reporter speech. "Means it's hush. In other words—newsworthy."

"Newsworthy?" Bella repeated.

"Don't get any ideas, Mr. Newlin," the officer, cautioned. "M and G trains aren't running this morning and we're supposed to keep that fact top-secret quiet. No media reports. Good thing it's a weekend."

"M and G trains cross the park, north-south and east-west." Lyman took mental notes. His blood turned warm and began pumping through his veins at warp speed. Lyman looked out the window. But his racing mind was elsewhere.

"You're sure familiar with the city subway system," the officer observed. "Probably grew up here. I'm originally from Canada." The policeman spoke into his rearview mirror. "Being a newspaper reporter, Mr. Newlin, what's the most interesting you know about New City?"

Lyman didn't hear the officer's question.

"Too hard to think of one thing?" The policeman took a gulp of his coffee. "How come Moonrocks store-brewed coffee stays hot so much longer than coffee I make at home? Ever notice that?"

"Because it costs six bucks a cup!" Bella shrieked. "It better stay hot!"

"Mrs. Stella lives midtown," Lyman said, returning from his distraction. "Can you drop us off at the next exit? I'll see she gets home and then I'll take a cab back to the *Chronicle*."

"I don't live—" Bella attempted to protest.

Lyman squeezed her hand.

"Not a problem," the officer replied. "Be my pleasure." He flicked on the turning signal and merged into the right lane.

"You promised," Bella grumbled. "I don't like changes—"

"Made to your plans." Lyman finished the sentence with a whisper. "I need this story, Bella." He looked into her eyes.

Mama Stella's glowering glare softened.

"Please?" Lyman pressed his knee against Bella's.

"Oh, whatever!" Bella scooted away, but not immediately.

"Thank you," Lyman whispered. "I owe you one." He gave her a quick wink and an affectionate smile.

Bella snatched the blanket and turned towards the window. She stared into the snowy distance.

Widowed, childless Clarabella Stella sighed and cracked a bittersweet smile.

Chapter 18

NEVER MIND

Sevlow's flashlight beam illuminated the way through the maze of tunnels beneath Midtown Gardens Park. The pack followed behind the white-haired alpha wolf as Mighty Mouse sang the opening lyrics from HI HO, over and over.

"Hi-ho, hi-ho, it's off to work we go, hi-ho, hi-ho, hi-ho, hi-ho, hi-ho, hi-ho… Hi-ho, hi-ho, it's off to work we go, hi-ho, hi-ho, hi-ho, hi-ho, hi-ho, hi-ho…"

"Something's missing," Dragon said, interrupting the repetitive tune.

"Yeah. The next verse of that annoying song." TJ covered his ears.

"Besides that," Dragon replied. He nudged Mighty Mouse.

"I was waiting for one of you to mention it," Sevlow remarked.

"We forget some supplies?" Seamus asked. He hoped he hadn't overlooked anything. Seamus pulled off his backpack and took a quick inventory.

"Benjamin usually serenades us with his signature song," Sevlow said.

Seamus breathed a sigh of relief. He zipped his gear bag and slung it back over his shoulders. "Signature song? I thought Mighty Mouse was trying to shut down our brains before we met the beelzebubbles."

"Yeah, we've gotta have the right song," said TJ. "What's a

mission without it?"

Mighty Mouse pointed at Seamus and whispered to Dragon.

"Don't worry. He won't laugh," Dragon assured.

"Me? Laugh?" Seamus said. "When I was a kid I used to get up in front of people and sing, all the time. Isn't that true, Sir?"

"That is a fact. 'The Kids Last Fight' was Seamus's favorite song," Sevlow replied. "He sang it at every social gathering. Whether he was requested to do so or not."   Seamus cleared his throat and burst into song. "It was Tiger Wilson versus Kid McCoy in the summer of '93. Now the Kid was everybody's pride and joy, just as game as a kid could be. With his darlin' Bess in the second row..."

Mighty Mouse giggled and snorted.

"Now who's making fun?" Seamus teased. "It's your turn. Go ahead."

"Mister Trouble never hangs around," crooned the littlest werewolf in a baby baritone. "When he hears this mighty sound. Here I come to save the day. That means that Mighty Mouse is on his way. Yes, sir when there is wrong to right. Mighty Mouse will join the fight. On the sea or on the land, he's got the situation well in hand." He took an exaggerated bow.

High-fives followed.

Dragon whistled and clapped. "Encore!"

"I'm guessing these beelzebubbles don't have ears," Seamus observed. "We're not exactly the quiet bunch."

Mighty Mouse let out a loud playful howl, "AWOOOO!"

The jubilant mood was shifted by an observation.

"Hey, what's that?" TJ said, pointing.

"Where?" asked Mighty Mouse, scurrying to the front of the pack. "I want to see. I can't see anything."

TJ shined his flashlight on a furry lump in the brief distance. "It looks like an animal." He jogged ahead to investigate.

The others followed.

TJ knelt beside a black and white dog. The hound was splattered with mud. A bloody gash along its rib cage oozed and his leg was bent in an unnatural position.

"Is it dead?" Mighty Mouse stroked the hound. "What happened? How'd he get down here?"

"I don't know." TJ examined the dog's wound.

The hound blinked.

"He's alive!" Mighty Mouse shouted.

"Hi, boy." TJ's voice was soothing. "Don't worry. We'll get you outta here."

"TJ," Sevlow cautioned. "There's no time to attend to him at present. We'll return afterward and see to his care."

The dog whimpered and licked TJ's hand.

"Sir," TJ pleaded. "Maybe the little guy lives nearby." TJ pointed up. "A subway grate. The roads are slick. I bet he got hit by a car and was knocked through the opening."

"TJ's probably right," Dragon said. "Looks like a car hit him broadside."

"Sevlow, I can take him home and meet back up with you." TJ shined his flashlight on the dog's collar tag. "Liberace, 1 City Avenue, (212) 555-"

Seamus interrupted. "1 City Avenue? That's the Mayor's address, Tracie Mansion. The mayor has a black and white dog. He takes that hound everywhere. Bet Fink's going nuts looking for him."

"Maybe there's a reward too," Mighty Mouse said. "It's gotta be the Mayor's dog."

Liberace thumped his tail.

"See," TJ said. "The little guy knows he's been identified. Let me take him back to the mayor, Sir. I'll be quick."

"TJ, your compassion is your virtue and your vice." Sevlow shook his head and gave a solemn warning. "You said yourself, the pack should stay together."

"Pleeeeease!" Mighty Mouse begged on his friend's behalf.

"We forget injuries, but never kindnesses," Dragon reminded.

"Liberace is privileged to have so many steadfast allies." Sevlow checked his GPS before rendering a verdict. "You understand, TJ, I do not, with a clear conscience, condone separating from the pack."

"That means we're near Tracie Mansion and you're going to give me permission to take Liberace home." TJ grinned. "Two hundred years is a very long time, Sir."

"Yes, TJ, it is." There was a warm reluctance in Sevlow's voice.

TJ lifted Liberace. The hound looked small lying in TJ's massive arms. "I'll be back with the pack before you miss me."

Sevlow smiled at TJ and then motioned for the rest of the

pack to move out. "We must depart at once."

They headed south.

"Hey, Boss." TJ called. "I just want you to know something."

"Know?" Sevlow repeated.

TJ fixed his gaze on the white-haired werewolf. "You're an angel." He flashed an affectionate grin and walked into the darkness.

Bella and Lyman stood on the deserted station platform of the G train's Midtown Gardens subway stop.

"Now what?" Bella was getting impatient.

"We jump down onto the tracks and head into the tunnel," Lyman instructed.

"Oh no!" Mama Stella protested. "First you make me sleep in a tollbooth, now you want me to leap onto subway tracks. You're nuts! I changed my mind about this investigative reporter crap. Take me home."

"You heard those voices too." Lyman sat himself on the edge of the redlined platform. He was a man on a mission. "Something secret is going on in that tunnel and I aim to find out what it is." He swung his dangling legs forward and plopped down onto the gravel below.

"It's pitch black in there," Bella said. "You don't even have a flashlight. What if the mayor turns the trains back on? You're gonna get squished!"

"It was selfish of me to invite you," Lyman said. "I'm sorry.

183

It's just that I enjoy the sound of your voice and your wonderful company."

"Oh, alright," Bella snarled. She sat herself across from him on the dirty subway platform ledge. She folded her arms and surveyed the situation.

Lyman smiled. "It may be dangerous. If you prefer to stay here alone on a deserted subway platform, I promise I'll come back for you when I'm done."

"Oh, shut up!" Bella shouted. "Gimme a chance to get my nerve up. I hate heights."

Lyman held out a helping hand.

Bella ignored Lyman's attempted assistance. Mama Stella rolled onto her belly and slid off the platform. Her feet made a *chhh* sound when they touched the gray gravel below. She released her straining outstretched arms, steadied her footing, and dusted herself off. "You'd better win some sorta prize for this darn story."

Lyman hooked his arm through hers. "I think I just did."

Claudia removed the flashlight and a bottled water from her satchel. She shook a splash of water onto each of her hands and then dried them on a fresh strip of toilet paper. "Gross!" Simon reappeared just as Claudia was disposing of the wet wad. One forceful fling and the white clump stuck to the crumbling ceiling above. "I've always wanted to do that." Claudia tripped on something while stepping back to admire her handiwork. She caught herself before falling. Claudia held her lantern over the box. It was a cardboard container labeled *Pyrotechnics*.

184

"Miss, Claudia," Simon said, gliding in excited circles. "My brother Benjamin is walking with the big dogs, and there's a new one."

"I won't ask why your brother walks his dogs underground," Claudia replied, in much better humor than when Simon departed. "But if he walked in here with dogs, he can walk back out too." She adjusted the lantern beam to high. "Take me to Benjamin." She stepped over the box.

"You want to meet my brother, now?" Simon asked.

"Yes, Simon, I want to meet your brother Benjamin the singing dog walker and I want to get the heck out of these grimy tunnels." Claudia guzzled down the rest of the water she was holding. She placed the empty plastic bottle into her supply satchel. "I'm ready, lead the way!"

The way was blocked by two familiar figures.

"Mami! Papi!" Claudia shouted. "I have been calling you! Where have you been? Why didn't you come?"

"We are here now, *mi'ja*" Salvador said. "We heard your calling, but your mami and I have been very busy."

"¡*Qué muñeco*!" Paz cooed. "Claudia, who is this little doll?"

"Mami, Papi, this is Simon. He helped me escape from a locked tomb." There was a hint of childish whine in Claudia's voice. She folded her arms. "You've been very busy? Did you have any idea that a werewolf kidnapped me and locked me in a cold scary bathroom-less dungeon, *con muertas*?"

"*Sí*, and you met a friend in the dungeon of dead persons," Paz observed.

185

"Mami!" Claudia cried. "You act like you don't care."

"Claudia," Salvador comforted in a reassuring tone. "My poor daughter, you must have been very frightened in the tomb, even with a little boy to keep you company, but Sevlow meant you no harm. It was for your own safety."

"Sevlow? I didn't say his name. How do you know Sevlow?" Claudia's wide eyes betrayed her astonishment. "Do you know Seamus too?"

"*Lobo sueño?*" Paz replied. "He is your dream wolf."

"How?" Claudia looked from one parent to another. "You said you couldn't tell me about my wolf dreams, when all along you knew about Seamus?"

"We could not speak about your dreams, about the wolf because the time was too soon," Paz said in firm-mother tone. "*Mi amor*, your father and I did not lie. There is a difference."

"That's still not fair," Claudia cried. "It's my life, you know!"

"Spoken like a true teenager." Salvador laughed.

Claudia couldn't help herself; she grinned at her father.

"Do not criticize our silence," Salvador continued. "There is much your mami and I have witnessed and discovered on the other side, more than we are permitted to share. Even with you, *mi'ja*."

"Are there any other secrets you're keeping from me?" asked Claudia.

"Claudia," Salvador said. "We have been protecting you and helping *los lobos*."

"Helping the wolves?" asked Claudia. "Seamus and

Sevlow?"

"*Mas*," Paz replied.

"More werewolves?" Claudia shook her head. "So, I was right. The motorcycle thief was a werewolf too."

"*Sí, hay cinco*," Salvador said. "It is now necessary for you to also protect them."

"From a little fat man," Paz added. "*Y una vieja loca*,"

"*¿De quién?*" Claudia was not thoroughly confused. "A small fat man and a crazy old woman? They're after Seamus and the other werewolves?"

"Miss Claudia," Simon interrupted the family chatter. "Do you still want to go see my brother Benjamin?"

"I'm sorry, Simon." Claudia was. "I don't have time to meet your brother. But I want to, just later. Right now I have to help my parents, and I need to help Seamus. He's the friend I told you about."

Simon lowered his head in disappointment and sulked "But Seamus is Benjamin's friend too," Simon mumbled.

Paz and Salvador gave one another a surprised look.

Claudia's mind was on Seamus, and what else her parents may or may not know. "What did you say, Simon?"

Simon turned away. "Never mind, Miss."

Salvador changed the subject. "You may join us, Simon. Would you like to help the wolves?"

The little ghost beamed, "Yes, Sir!"

"*¡Vamos!*" Paz waved her hand. "*Los dos locos* have already found their way here to the tunnels."

"Who are the two crazies? You still haven't explained anything to me," Claudia reminded *los padres*. "Who are they after? And how do I help Seamus and the other werewolves?"

"Your papi will talk to you along the way," Paz assured her. "Begin, Salvador, tell her about Mickey *y el jardín vegetal de muertos*."

"Mickey and the dead vegetable garden?" Claudia was now completely confused. "What do dead vegetables have to do with any of this?"

"Claudia," Salvador replied. "Soon enough, your mami and I will explain everything that you are permitted to know."

Paz, Salvador, Claudia, and Simon hurried down the left corridor.

A few moments later another group arrived at the fork in the road.

Chapter 19

NO GOOD DEED GOES UNPUNISHED

Sevlow slipped into the subway tunnel alcove and checked his watch. "Thirty seconds. Secure."

Seamus, Dragon, and Mighty Mouse fell into line and tucked their bodies against the arched passageway wall.

Seamus braced himself in anticipation of the train's impending air gust and intense vibration. He closed his eyes and waited for the G to pass.

It never arrived.

"Maybe I got it wrong," Dragon said, rereading a folded timetable card. "Nope, right here, says Sunday. Even in this weather, trains should be running close to schedule."

Sevlow didn't reply. He entered a set of coordinates into his GPS. A map flashed across the screen. "Follow me." He left his position and traversed the double tracks.

The pack stepped over the subway rails and followed Sevlow along a narrow dimly lit service walkway that led into another silent tunnel.

Sevlow knelt down and placed a hand on one of the steel tracks. He checked his GPS again before shining a light into the deserted corridor. "Neither the G nor the M appears to be operating."

"Gaffney messed up," Dragon said in a-matter-of-fact tone. "Made the call before Sevlow gave the order."

"No way," Seamus defended. "Sarge stuck to the plan. Believe me."

"I agree," Sevlow said. "Sergeant Gaffney is steadfast." Sevlow removed the 2-way radio from his pocket. Before he could summon, a voice crackled over the receiver.

"Sevlow… Sevlow, it's Gaffney. Do you read? Over."

Even with the flawed connection, Seamus could hear the urgency in Sergeant Gaffney's voice.

"This is Sevlow. Over."

"Sevlow, we've got a situation. Over."

The leader nodded in agreement. "G and M service has been halted. Over."

"Affirmative. I just found out Fink turned off the G and M trains," Gaffney relayed amid static. "He called-in a 10-58. Over."

"Did the mayor enlist support? Over," Sevlow replied.

"Negative," the Sarge said. "It's a hands-off. A-typical. Over."

"Why didn't Gaffney tell us sooner," Dragon muttered, rubbing his spiky hair.

"He's been busy. Anyway, 10-58's aren't continuously broadcast," Seamus defended. "High security transmissions on a need-to-know basis."

Sevlow held up his hand and motioned for silence.

Dragon and Seamus heeded the command.

"Should I meet up with you? Over," the Sarge asked.

"Negative," Sevlow replied. "Man your position and keep me apprised of any additional developments. Over."

"Roger. Over and out." Sarge's voice faded to silence.

Sevlow slid the radio back into his pocket. His attention was drawn to an object on the ground. He picked up a cardboard tube and appeared to be lost in thought.

"Maybe the mayor turned off the trains because his dog's missing," Mighty Mouse said, breaking the pensive quiet. "Maybe Mr. Fink's down here too?"

"Very astute observation, Benjamin." Sevlow complimented the littlest werewolf. "Yet that hypothesis neither explains the absence of a search party nor Mayor Fink's deliberate secrecy."

"Mayor Fink would have every free officer in these tunnels with beefy treats, yelling, 'Liberace!' It doesn't make sense." Seamus's remark was interrupted by a faint but foul odor. "Arrgh! What is that?" he gagged.

"A small number of beelzebubbles have passed this way," Sevlow noted with marked urgency. "Their portal has been opened." He sniffed the canister he was holding. "I detect something else as well."

"But TJ," Dragon said. "He—"

Sevlow interjected. "Yes, TJ's safety may have been compromised." The leader thought for a brief moment. "Dragon, Benjamin, you remain with me. Seamus, I'm tasking you with reconnaissance. Do your best to hold human form in case Sergeant Gaffney has any new developments to report." Sevlow handed Seamus the GPS and 2-way radio. "My fur coat doesn't contain pockets." Sevlow flashed a quick grin.

"While in werewolf form we can communicate telepathically with one another," Dragon added.

Seamus could see disappointment written across Dragon's face as he spoke. He felt a glint of privilege that Sevlow had chosen him, the rookie, to recover TJ.

"If TJ has been seized you will need to release him." Sevlow spoke with resolve. "Time is of the essence."

"If TJ's under the beelzebubbles' spell." Dragon took charge of the directives. "You're going to have to go inside his head. You need to alter the possessing memory."

"Alter a memory?" Seamus forgot his short-lived pride. "How?"

"Sir," Dragon pleaded. "To send an untaught man into battle is to cast him away." Dragon lowered his gaze. "Please, let me go instead."

"Dragon, I share your profound concern for TJ's welfare." Sevlow said. "However, rounding up the beelzebubbles, especially if they have taken human hostages, and closing the portal will require a group effort. Your experience and dexterity are essential."

Dragon bowed.

Seamus wished he'd been born a werewolf or at the very least been given a 'How to be a Werewolf' manual.

"Neophyte countenance betrays your reticence," Sevlow observed.

"Think that means I look like it's my first time in the ring and I'm sweating bullets," Seamus summed up Sevlow's observation. *Wonder if he regrets changing me?*

"I have not been disappointed," Sevlow replied. "I have confidence in your courage and readiness."

Seamus felt a wave of adrenaline surge through his veins, replacing trepidation with gusto. His vision blurred. Seamus shook his head and focused every bit of his being on a single word: *Claudia.*

"Stay alert!" Dragon snapped. "Whatever you do, don't speak to a beelzebubble, regardless of their form," Dragon coached. "You can't talk and secure your thoughts at the same time. If TJ's under, stare through his eyes, into his mind. Let yourself enter TJ's memory, but no matter what you see, don't freak out and change. It's TJ's recollection, not yours." Dragon paused. He took a breath before continuing in a more supportive voice. "You can do it, Seamus. Hold your temper and think strong."

"Drift into TJ's mind?" Seamus shook his head. "I don't understand half of this undead mission business," he confessed.

"Seamus," Sevlow assured. "Werewolf instincts will guide your actions. Follow them, without hesitation."

"Got it?" Dragon asked.

"Yeah, I got it." Seamus hoped he did.

TJ walked along the deserted subway station toward the City Avenue exit. He cradled Liberace in his arms. "Almost home, boy."

"L-i-b-e-r-a-c-e…" a faint voice echoed through the darkness behind them.

The hound whimpered.

"You heard it too." TJ turned around and retraced his last few steps. "Hello? Someone there?" he called.

"H-e-l-p …" This time the resonating voice was a bit stronger.

TJ squatted at the edge of the subway platform and hollered into the tunnel. "Who's there?"

"W-h-o-s t-h-e-r-e…" TJ's own words echoed back.

There was a loud THUD from somewhere just beyond the bend.

"Hey! You OK?"

Silence.

"Ah, man." TJ let out a sigh and stood. "I'm sorry, fella. You're gonna have to give me a minute. Someone else needs help."

Liberace thumped his tail against TJ's chest.

"You recognize the voice." TJ set Liberace down atop a graffiti-covered commuter bench. He took off his backpack and removed his black T-shirt. TJ placed the tee across the hound's wounded flank.

Liberace sneezed.

"Yeah, the shirt smells like wet dog." TJ laughed. "If Sevlow comes by don't rat me out." TJ stroked Liberace's chin. "I'll get you home to your master soon, promise."

Liberace's big brown eyes fixed on TJ. He let out a weak but affectionate cry.

TJ removed a flashlight from his pack and then threw the gear bag back over his broad bare shoulder. For a split second, TJ thought he'd heard his name called. But there was no time to confirm; he leapt onto the subway tracks and sprinted into the darkness.

Bella and Lyman arrived at the fork in the tunnel, still arm-in-arm. A lone flickering light bulb cast two long entwined shadows against the crumbling tile wall.

Bella hesitated and sniffed the air. "I smell firecrackers."

Lyman sniffed. "Maybe it's escaped exhaust fumes. The Washington Tunnel is beneath here somewhere."

"I know firecrackers when I smell them," Bella insisted. "Cannon Balls, M-80's, Cherry Bombs, Mickey was always blowing things up."

"That kid sounds like a hand full." Lyman said, although he kept additional Mickey criticisms to himself. "Choose a path, left or right?"

"How the heck am I supposed to tell which way we should go?"

"Well then, Liberal or Conservative?" Lyman asked. "What side of the aisle are you on politically?"

"I voted for Fink," Bella growled. "And I'm sorry I did. Ruby red fire hydrants and pooper-scooper bags on every corner, what a waste of taxpayer money when the city's bridges and tunnels are falling apart. He's a dog-loving weirdo!"

"So it's settled," Lyman concluded. "We take your pick, and go the other way."

Seamus ran along the M tracks towards the City Avenue station. His mind was a web of focused confusion. Seamus feared that five years of full moons and anger episodes hadn't prepared him for his current werewolf duties. On the other hand, he was having the time of his undead life. The previous 24 hours replayed in Seamus's brain like a hard rockin' music video. Making out with the hot girl was the catchy hook.

Seamus was about to hit reverie rewind when his wolf ears tuned into a faint whimper resonating through the corridor.

"Liberace…"

"TJ!" Seamus called. He stopped running and waited for his teammate's answer.

The darkness returned an unexpected response.

Seamus's voice seeped into a neighboring tunnel, catching the attention of friendly ears.

"Seamus! It's me, Claudia!" Claudia returned a welcoming cry. "Seamus, I'm over here!"

"Claudia! Where are you?"

Claudia sprinted in the direction of Seamus's voice. "Keep talking, Seamus. I'll find you!"

Three gliding ghosts kept pace at Claudia's heels. Two of the three weren't looking very pleased about the change of plans.

"No, Claudia!" Paz shouted. "¡*Ignórelo*!"

"Ignore him?" Claudia questioned, not slowing her gait.

"Yes, do not see the wolf," Salvador said.

"It's way too late for that!" Claudia called to her parents. "Seamus and I are meant to be together, and you two know it!"

"Yes, but do not go to him now," her father implored.

"Claudia, you have important work to do, and so does Seamus!" Paz's tone was more insistent.

"I can't wait, so please don't try and stop me!" Claudia hurdled over a pile of rubble. "I need to see him, just for a minute."

Salvador threw up his floating hands in defeat.

Claudia heard gravel crunching beneath shoes. The sound was getting closer. "Seamus!" Any apprehensions Claudia had about defying her parents vanished as soon as she saw Seamus emerge from the shadows.

"Claudia!"

Claudia flung herself into Seamus's open arms. "Oh, Seamus! I—"

Claudia's next words were devoured by Seamus's kiss.

Claudia disregarded the fact that Simon and *los padres* were watching and gave herself to the moment. She closed her eyes and released all disagreeable reminders of the last 24 hours. Her body thawed and her blistered feet no longer ached and throbbed.

"I'm so sorry," Seamus whispered, before planting a second kiss.

Claudia pulled away. "Sorry for what?"

"That Sevlow locked you up," Seamus said. "But it was for your own good."

"For my own good," Claudia repeated. "How come everyone thinks it was—"

"NO!"

Claudia's sentence was interrupted by a distant shout. "What was that?"

"TJ." Seamus said with urgency.

"Another werewolf?" Claudia asked.

"Yeah, the guy who stole my bike," Seamus said on the fly. "I think he's in danger, maybe separated from Liberace."

Claudia chased after him. She was losing ground. "How can I help?"

Seamus hollered back to her. "Look for Liberace, an injured dog. Try the City Avenue station. Get him to a vet, and then go home. Stay out of these tunnels." Seamus broke into a high-speed dash and was soon out of view.

Claudia stopped running. She put her hands on her hips and bent over.

Simon floated beside her.

"Simon." Claudia grimaced. "Remind me to never again run in riding boots. My blisters now have blisters."

"Miss Claudia, Seamus is Benjamin's friend too," the little ghost said.

A light bulb went off in Claudia's head. She recited Simon's words. "Benjamin plays with big dogs." She righted herself. "Simon, why didn't I figure it out sooner? Your brother is one of the five werewolves."

"Yes, Miss," Simon replied. "My brother didn't die from coughing, like me."

Things were beginning to make sense to Claudia.

"C'mon!" she exclaimed. "We have to help Seamus and TJ and a dog named Liberace!" She looked around. "Mami, Papi?"

Los padres were gone.

The mayor stood in the dank tunnel. Blood oozed from a fresh gash above his left eyebrow. There was a red smear on the wall beside him. He stared like a statue into an indiscernible void.

TJ sniffed the air. "Your Honor?" TJ approached with care. He reached into his backpack and removed a ski cap. "Press this against your head to stop the bleeding." TJ held out the woolen cover. "That bad smell is coming from something very dangerous. I've gotta get you outta here. Your dog is hurt, but alive. I'll take you both home."

"That talking fool would not stop waking up and calling to his hound." An icy smile slithered across fake Fink's face. "He's finally unconscious."

"Huh?" before TJ could react, a burping beelzebubble ambushed him from behind. TJ's eyes fluttered in their sockets and his body began to twitch and jerk. He fought to focus on his mantra and thwart the memory that was commandeering his mind.

The stupefied house staff stepped out of the shadows.

"After my little fireworks display," fake Fink declared. "New City will be in a frenzied panic and I'll have no further use for the mayor and his staff." He leaned close to TJ's contorting face. "For an encore perhaps I should lead a group suicide."

"NO!" TJ shouted, just before a grim childhood memory consumed him.

"Tom!" A stout sweaty woman in a soiled apron stood outside of the kitchen house and shouted towards the fields. "TJ, you little ox, where you run off ta?" She waited for a moment then wiped her moist ebony face across her muscular forearm. "You want me tellin' yor mama she need be fetching you agin? TOM!"

Tom crouched beside an unhitched wagon, waiting for his chance to trade afternoon chores for a summer swim. After a short time his auntie gave up the futile calling and returned to her cooking duties. Tom looked around—the coast was clear. He slipped into the fields and sprinted away from the protected grounds of his home, towards ten-year-old independence.

With clothes safely stashed behind a bush, Tom cracked off a segment of hollow reed, stuck it in his mouth, and eased himself into the big pond. The cool water rippled away from Tom's sinking naked body. He knelt, completely submerged, on the soggy shore bottom. Tom posed, his arms outstretched and fingers spread, still as a tree trunk. He waited for an unsuspecting fish to pass between his palms. He aimed to catch one with his bare hands like some of the older boys bragged they could.

Tom clamped his front teeth against the reed that protruded at an angle through the water's surface. He breathed through his mouth, without releasing any air bubbles. Tom watched through a haze of water as a procession of little catfish swam past his fingers. One-by-one the curious fish approached the intruder, and then bolted away, only to return again for another, closer peek.

SPLASH!

The calm of the moment was shattered.

Tom retreated into the tall foliage along the shore behind him. He stifled his breathing and watched.

"Nigger went this a way," a man's voice shouted in the approaching distance.

A black man lifted his head out from under the water and panted. Tom could see the terror in his eyes. The man floundered and sank. Tom knew the man was in grave danger; he was a pursued runaway who couldn't swim. Tom's helping heart trumped his *stay safe* thoughts. He broke off another strip of reed and left his cover. The man scrambled to the surface for a second time.

"Missa," Tom called in a hushed tone as he paddled. "Missa, gimme yor hand."

The man grabbed onto the boy's extended arm.

"You kin hide over dere." Tom pointed to the shore cover. "Put dis in yor mouf." He passed the man a reed. "Breaf," he instructed.

The lesson was cut short by a shot bouncing off the surface of the pond.

"We got us two niggers!" a second man yelled. "Two runaway niggers in thair tryin' ta escape!"

201

The following gun blast did not miss its mark. It blew off the back of the runaway's head. The force of the fire sent his lifeless body crashing into Tom.

They plunged together into the depths of the pond.

The water around Tom was laden with brain matter and crimson with blood. His thrashing leg caught in the dead man's rope belt. Tom couldn't release himself. He couldn't breath. He choked. His lungs filled with water. Tom was drowning.

Chapter 20

HELL AND A HANDBAG

The Dynamic Duo headed right, down the deserted tunnel. Bella clutched Lyman's arm on one side and her handbag on the other as they negotiated together through near darkness.

"I don't hear anything," Bella complained. "We should have gone the other way."

"If we don't find anyone soon, we'll turn back," Lyman promised. "Are you sure you don't have a match or a lighter in your handbag? I'd have a better idea where we were headed if I could just see something."

Bella unzipped her purse and rummaged through the contents without the benefit of sight. "I don't feel anything that resembles a lighter. I told you, Mickey probably threw it out. It was OK for him to smoke, but not me. I—"

Lyman stumbled on a hunk of cement and knocked himself and Bella off balance, cutting off her sentence and sending the open purse flying through the air. The contents dispersed into the abyss like confetti from a party-popper.

"You idiot!" Bella cried, scrambling in the blackness for her belongings.

"What?" Lyman asked what he already knew. "Did you drop something?"

"Did I drop something?" Bella wailed. "You tripped, you big oaf, and made me fling my handbag!" She swung her clenched fist through the air and connected with Lyman's bent elbow.

"OW!" Lyman yelled.

"Ouch!" Bella screamed. "You made me hurt my knuckle."

Lyman took a step backwards in anticipation of another invisible right-hook. He tumbled over the same chunk of concrete. This time it dislodged.

BURP! A putrid cloud escaped from under the block.

"Lyman, you old poop!" Bella gagged.

"I thought it was you," Lyman replied, ducking.

"Me?" Mama Stella answered with indignation. "I didn't fart!"

"Well, it wasn't me," Lyman gagged. "ARGH!" he grabbed hold of his nose.

"Well if it wasn't me or you, then what the hell made that stinking sound?" The smell intensified. Bella covered her nose and mouth with her free forearm. "Shake a leg. I bet a sewer main broke." She clutched Lyman's hand. "Gas is escaping!"

Something wrapped around Lyman's ankle. He jiggled his leg. A soft object went flying through the darkness and landed atop the opening that was once obstructed by the cement block. Lyman realized he'd hurled Bella's handbag. He kept the fact to himself.

The handbag containing its last remaining item fell into the smelly chasm.

"You're not really supposed to shake a leg!" Bella snapped. "You're going to knock me over!"

"Sorry." Lyman yanked Mama Stella along.

"But my handbag," Bella protested, trying to keep pace with Lyman. "I'm not leaving without my handbag!"

"I promise." Lyman pulled Bella. "I'll get a flashlight and come back here and find your purse."

"And everything that was in it!" Mama Stella demanded. "My wallet, my keys, my favorite lipstick, and Mickey's first communion picture!"

"All of it," Lyman guaranteed. "But right now we have to get out of here."

The sound of Lyman and Bella's retreating feet prevented them from hearing a strong sucking sound. The fusty force pulled the handbag containing Mickey's photograph. Down it was sucked, down, down, down.

S-E-A-R-C-H-I-N-G...

The illuminated nine letters traveled across Alex's cell phone display. "I still can't get any service."

"We're in the boonies," the cabbie replied. "But there's gotta be a gas station along this road. The sign on the highway said food and diesel. This tank doesn't run on regular."

"Maybe they'll have a pay phone." Alex set down his cell and lowered and raised the passenger window to remove a covering of ice that was obstructing his outside view.

"We've been on the road for hours." The cabbie rubbed his stomach. "I could go for something in my tank too. How about you?"

Alex didn't respond.

"I can't believe this weather. It just won't let up," the cabbie commented, increasing the wiper tempo. "Gotta make the record books, a foot of snow in April?"

The driver glanced into his rearview mirror.

Alex was staring through the side glass.

"We're an hour from New City," the cabbie said in a reassuring tone. "Bet your sister's home by now, safe and sound."

Alex nodded and returned an uneasy smile.

Claudia and Simon made their way to the City Avenue station. Claudia spotted Liberace on the bench where TJ had left him. She hoisted herself up, climbed onto the subway platform, and rushed to the hound. Simon glided beside her. "Seamus was right." Claudia stroked the dog. "Hi, Liberace. Poor little guy."

"The doggie is so cute," Simon cooed.

Liberace thumped his tail.

"I believe he can hear you," Claudia said. "My cat, Misha knows when *los padres* are in the room." She scratched Liberace's head.

"Why's Liberace wearing a shirt?" Simon asked, hovering between the slats of the soiled commuter bench.

"Maybe TJ covered him?" Claudia lifted the black tee. "Oh, my gosh!" She let the shirt drop and took a composing breath.

"Why's he bleeding?" Simon looked as if he were about to cry. "Is he going to die if you don't fix him?"

"He's stayed alive this long so I bet he'll be OK." Claudia was trying to reassure herself as much as Simon. She removed the

burlap satchel from her back. "I have a first-aid kit and water."
Claudia pulled a bottle from her supply bag and unscrewed the cap.
"Simon, remember how you held the fork and chopped stones and
helped me escape from the creepy tomb?"

"Yes, Miss Claudia," Simon nodded.

"I need you to hold this bottle so Liberace can have a drink.
It'll make him feel better." She handed Simon the water.

He gripped the plastic container with both misty hands.
Simon placed the floating water in front of the dog.

Liberace licked the mouth of the bottle.

"He likes it!" Simon exclaimed.

"Good boy." Claudia set the opened first-aid kit down on
the bench next to the hound. "Simon, you keep Liberace drinking,
and I'll clean his cut." She opened another water bottle and doused
a wad of gauze. Claudia gritted her teeth, lifted the tee, and
examined the wound. "Urgh," she wiped away a sticky glob of
blood from Liberace's fur.

The dog whimpered.

"You'll be alright," Simon whispered.

It appeared to Claudia that the blood on the gash had begun
to coagulate.

"Miss Claudia is a nice lady," Simon said. "She's going to
help you get all better so you don't die, like me."

"Oh, Simon," Claudia's heart ached for the creature and the
child. "I wish you hadn't died from the cough. I know that was so
horrible for you to leave your life so soon, to leave Benjamin."

"It wasn't fair."

"No, it wasn't fair," Claudia agreed. She finished dabbing the wound and applied a covering of anti-bacterial ointment. "But the good part is you were able to follow your brother around for all these years. And you met me. I don't know what I would have done without your help and your company."

"Really, Miss?" Simon smiled.

"Really," Claudia returned the grin. "My parents told me that love is an eternal protective force."

Simon gave Claudia a blank stare.

"For instance," Claudia explained. "Saving Liberace and helping me escape from the tomb wouldn't have been possible if you'd lived a long life, and died an old man. So, good came from bad. Right?

"Right!" Simon shouted. "And it's a good thing Benjamin rips up bad people!"

Claudia recalled Mickey's recent decapitation and guts munching. Her optimistic mood took a woozy dive. She gagged and swallowed hard.

"Are you getting sick, Miss Claudia?"

Claudia refocused her attention on Liberace. The visual wasn't much better. "I'll be OK, Simon." She removed a rolled bandage from the first-aid kit. "I'm going to wrap Liberace's belly. Then we'll leave," Claudia pointed towards the exit stairs. "I think we're close to the stables where I keep Pirate, my horse. Someone there will know what to do."

The dog whimpered.

"I'm sorry, boy," Claudia responded in kind.

"Why doesn't he stand up?" Simon asked. "Are his legs broken?"

"Maybe, but I think Liberace's not moving because his ribs are cracked," Claudia said. "Tilt the water bottle; see if he'll drink a little more."

Liberace's tongue missed the bottle and instead lapped Simon's hand. "He licked me!" the little ghost squealed.

"You felt that?" Claudia was surprised. She thought for a second. "Simon, you can't feel my touch but you can feel Liberace's."

Simon shrugged.

"When your brother is a werewolf, do you ever talk to him? Touch him? Call his name?" Claudia asked. "Does Benjamin know you're there?"

"I hide, but sometimes I think Benjamin sees me," Simon replied. "I want to talk to him, but I'm afraid. The big dogs might hear too and get mad at me."

Claudia secured Liberace's bandage and reached into her bag. She took out IL LUPO APPASSIONATO and opened to the bookmarked page. "Simon, I think I know a way that you and Benjamin can be together again, forever."

"Yeah!" Simon yelled. "I'm going to be with Benjamin! Simon and Benjamin!"

"Shh. Listen." Claudia scanned the passage. "What was your last name?"

"My name is Simon," the little ghost answered, sounding a bit confused.

"Simon what?" Claudia clarified. "The name after your first name. Like, my first name is Claudia and my last name is Peña. You and Benjamin also had last name. Think. Did Father Benedict ever call you by another name too?"

Simon's eyes shifted up and to the left. He was quiet for a moment.

"Smith, Jones," Claudia prompted.

"Allen!" Simon shouted. "Father would say, 'Master Allen' sometimes, sometimes when me and Benjamin didn't behave."

"Simon Allen," Claudia replied. "So your brother's name is Benjamin Allen. This book says if you go to your brother, and call his full name three times, while he's in werewolf form, it says he'll pass to the other side."

"Benjamin Allen, Benjamin Allen, Benjamin Allen," Simon practiced.

"Just like that, and Benjamin's werewolf days will be over," Claudia instructed. "That's what the books says. Sevlow marked this passage so maybe it's true that a mortal can send a werewolf to the other side. If you love him." Claudia shifted into sixth-sense and took an enlightened guess. "Simon, you waited for him all these years. Benjamin loves you too. Based on what my parents have said, I do believe whenever possible, love and fate mix together to make bad things good and sad things happy again." Liberace whimpered. His big brown blinking eyes were fixed on Claudia. She placed the book back into the satchel and slung it over her shoulders. "Benjamin doesn't have to stay a werewolf forever."

Simon cheered.

Claudia slid her arms carefully beneath Liberace's bandaged body. "Good boy," she lifted him off the bench. "Hold steady. We're going now."

Claudia made it to the third subway step before her exit was halted by a woman's shrill scream billowing from the tunnel.

"It's still after me!" hollered Bella, thrashing her arms about.

Lyman scurried behind her. "It's more than cold air. It's that *thing*; it followed us from the island!" He swiped at an invisible assailant.

Claudia saw *los padres* emerge from the tunnel along with the frenzied pair. Salvador and Paz floated in and out of Lyman and Bella, keeping them directed towards Claudia and Simon. *Los padres* seemed to be enjoying the ghostly round up.

Claudia couldn't help but chuckle aloud. "If you can't bring the mountain to Mohammed then bring Mohammed to the mountain."

"Who said that?" Bella shouted.

"Over here," Claudia called. "On the steps."

"Thank goodness," Lyman panted, still swiping at the air around him. "I was starting to think we'd never meet up with another person."

Los padres glided over to Claudia.

"Special delivery," Salvador announced with a flourishing hand.

"We have brought you the reporter and the mami." Paz in a more serious tone. "*¿Recuerda lo que tienes que decir?*"

"Yes, I remember what to say to them," Claudia assured her mother.

"What?" Lyman grunted, as he gave Mama Stella a boost onto the subway platform. "You say something?"

"I said my hands are full or I'd help you," Claudia lied.

"What do you got a dog for?" Bella growled. "There's no dogs allowed on trains. Unless it's a helper dog, and you don't look blind and he don't look very helpful to me."

Vieja loca, Claudia thought. "For your information, this is Mayor Fink's dog," Claudia replied, trying to sound authoritative. "And if you haven't noticed, the trains beneath Midtown Gardens Park have been shut off."

"We noticed," Lyman said, sitting on the edge of the filthy platform. "Word is Fink discontinued service." Lyman righted himself and dusted off his pants. "Mrs. Stella and I came down here to find out why."

"Because there's a serial killer on the loose," Claudia said, trying not to smirk. "The mayor has brought in a secret SWAT team to trap the murderer."

Drool formed on the sides of Lyman's mouth.

"A killer!" Bella screeched. "And you made me go in there!" Mama Stella took a swing at Lyman.

He avoided it, by centimeters.

"Stop it," Claudia said. "Listen, I know you're a reporter from the *Chronicle* and you're that missing Mickey's mother."

The dynamic duo looked stunned.

Bella spoke up. "How do—"

"No time for questions. But I'll make a deal with you. If you help me, I'll give you some inside information. Mr. Newlin, you'll be the first to break the big story."

"What?" Lyman was salivating. "What do you know about Mayor Fink's secret SWAT team?"

"I can't tell you about them, because I don't know, but I can tell you…" Claudia paused on purpose. The suspense made Lyman's eyes twitch. Claudia had her mother's sense of humor. "I know where the serial killer buried his victims."

"Where? Lyman's eyes were as wide a donuts. "Tell me!"

Claudia nodded towards Mama Stella. "In her vegetable garden."

Lyman gasped.

Bella fainted.

Los padres disappeared.

The sucking sound stopped. Mama Stella's handbag had arrived at its destination.

Chapter 21

NO PRESENT LIKE TIME

A rank cloud caught up with its leader and the stupefied house staff.

"Ah, so you've finally reached your destination," Fake Fink said to the smelly brown gyrating mist. "Take your places."

The beelzebubble cloud separated into five putrid pulsating bubbles; each took position inside one of the Mayor's caretakers. The employees morphed from lethargic to zombie lively.

Fake Fink scowled. "We could have done a more thorough set-up if you'd escaped on time. Back to the Washington Tunnel for adjustments after I make this call."

The mayor crossed the double rails and entered a connecting passageway. He walked over to an engineering booth located in an alcove along the service tunnel wall.

The foul five followed.

Fake Fink helped himself to the dial-less technician phone. The line rang as soon as the receiver was lifted from its cruddy cradle.

"Transportation. How may I direct your call?" A woman's voice escaped and echoed throughout the booth.

"Hello."

"Anyone there? I said how may I direct your call?" repeated the woman.

Grime clogged the mouthpiece. Fink spit on the receiver, wiped it across the mayor's pajama shirt, and placed the receiver on his ear. "Mayor Fink here," he replied, in a cool official tone. "Please inform your lead supervisor that G and M train service beneath Midtown Gardens should recommence... It means *start again*...Yes, Mayor Ed Fink... Executive order... F-I-N-K... I do not have to prove it... Then let me speak to your supervisor... Why not?...What do you mean he's just about to take his union-sanctioned cigarette break? ... I know what the word 'break' means!" The veins in Fake Finks' neck bulged. "I suppose I have no choice, but tell your boss this isn't an election year so there's no time like the present to clean house! ... It means the trains had better be back on in exactly 5 minutes, or else!" He slammed the receiver down and stormed out of the tiny booth.

Seamus found TJ alone, lying rigid and prone on the tunnel floor. TJ's mouth was twisted and contorted, his eyes fixed in a distant stare.

A nauseating wave of guilt hit Seamus. *What if I hadn't taken the Claudia detour?* "TJ." Seamus knelt beside his pack mate. "It's me, Seamus."

There was no reaction.

Seamus remembered Dragon's explicit instructions: *If TJ's under, clear your own thoughts and stare through his eyes, into his mind. Let yourself enter TJ's memory, but no matter what you see, don't freak out and change.*

Seamus stared into TJ's dilated pupils. There was only blackness beyond. After a few moments Seamus felt his mind's eye being directed forward, channeled into the hypnotic darkness

215

behind TJ's frozen gaze. Without warning, he found himself propelled into the scene playing inside TJ's head. Seamus was deep enough in the action to lose peripheral sight of the subway tunnel. He was so entrenched in the unfolding drama that he didn't feel the vibration in his side pocket, did not hear the familiar voice crackling across the airwaves, urgently beckoning for Sevlow, for someone, for *anyone* to answer.

"Darn!" Sarge placed the radio on his desk and rubbed his shiny head before reaching for the office phone. He pressed SPEAKER and dialed.

"You have reached the New City Department of Transportation," a woman's recorded voice said. "For English, press one. For Spanish press two. For Korean press three. For Swahili— "

The Sarge hit the one button.

"If you know your party's three-digit extension you may enter it at any time. To obtain a subway schedule press one-one. To report a problem press two-two. For Operations press three-three."

Sergeant Gaffney pressed three-three.

"Operations." The voice sounded a lot like the previous recording.

Sarge lifted the receiver. "This is police Sergeant Gaffney from the 20th precinct. Just received word that the G and M trains will resume running in 5 minutes… But more time is needed. … I understand, an executive order from Mayor Fink, but my undercover team is in those tunnels and they're presently in

216

danger, and out of *communicado*… It means I can't get in touch with them… Right, a life or death situation… Gimme more time to locate them… Yeah, well, if the mayor cleans house I'll probably be the first to go…. Another ten minutes, great. Thanks for the present." Sergeant Gaffney hung up, set the timer on his wristwatch, grabbed the radio, his hat, and headed out the door.

The westward gust sent a snow mound swirling in Claudia's direction. She tucked her chin down and cradled Liberace close to her chest before stepping from the sidewalk, over a white wall, and into the partially plowed street across from the subway station.

Simon hovered beside her, unhindered by the wicked weather.

Claudia squinted to the left and right. Not a vehicle or pedestrian in sight.

"It's a damn blizzard!" Bella exited close behind. She clutched her jacket and Lyman's hand. "Don't think I'm gonna walk anywhere in this storm!"

Liberace whimpered.

"Will you stop complaining," Claudia scolded. "You were a whole lot more pleasant while you were unconscious."

"Listen, you little brat!"

"Hey, hey, no more fighting." Lyman shielded his eyes from the white wind while assisting Bella over the frozen barricade.

217

"Little Red Riding Jacket started it," Mama Stella grumbled, kicking a snow clump out of her path.

"Yeah, right!" Claudia knew better.

"I said we'd help the lady and her dog," Lyman reminded in a soothing voice.

"You're so gullible," Bella scoffed. "She's lying about the murderer burying bodies in my garden. Mickey would a seen something. Her story is a big fat crock of—"

Lyman pressed his free hand over Mama Stella's mouth.

Claudia fought the urge to say what she *really* knew about Mickey. She bit her tongue and stuck to *los padres'* story. "Your son found out about the serial killer and tried to stop him. That's all I can tell you now."

"Miss Claudia, I see a car!" Simon called from above. "Coming this way!"

"There's a car headed in this direction," Claudia repeated.

"I don't see anything," Bella disputed. "She's imagining things again."

"Maybe we can hitch a ride and take Liberace to the stables." Claudia trekked two steps into the middle of the avenue.

"Why don't you drop Fink's dog at the 24/7 animal hospital near here?" Lyman suggested. "It's the best veterinary facility in the city, if not the country."

"Even better, thanks." Claudia could see the vehicle coming into view. "I think it's a taxi." She squinted harder. "But it's not the usual yellow."

218

"I'm not getting into any gypsy cab!" Mama Stella shouted. "They rob people!"

Lyman pulled Bella further into the street and waved his free hand. "Stop!"

A white and green Metro Cab pulled alongside the trio plus dog. The driver rolled down his window. "You guys stranded?"

"Metro Cab?" Mama Stella snapped. "There's no Metro Cab in New City."

"I'm from Bean Town. Had a crazy famous out-of-town fare. Can I give you guys a lift somewheres? But you're gonna have to direct me."

Bella opened the back door and hopped in. "229 Bleeker Place, Sicily Town."

"But first, New City Animal Hospital," Lyman slid in next to Bella. "Close to here. Left at the corner. Five blocks down on your right."

Mama Stella folded her arms and scowled.

Claudia carefully sat herself and Liberace on the edge of the bench seat beside Lyman. "The door won't close. She has to move over."

Bella didn't budge.

"Lady, scoot over. I can't drive with an open door," the cabbie said.

"Do you have any money?" Claudia asked Lyman. "I lost my purse."

"He lost my purse too," Mama Stella reminded. "Down in that dirty, dangerous subway tunnel he dragged me through. You said you were going to—"

The driver interrupted. "Hey, my last fare paid me more money than I made hauling passengers in the last six months. This time the ride's a present. Now move over lady so the missy and her hurt dog can get in and shut the door."

Bella grabbed the seat lip and held firm.

"Bella, move over," Lyman pleaded. "You're wasting valuable time."

"Last night I score by picking up Alejandro Peña; today it's paybacks with Cruella De Vil," the cabbie moaned.

"Who?" Claudia's ears perked.

"The mean lady from that Dalmatian dog movie."

"No, before that. You said Alejandro Peña." Claudia leaned over Lyman, into the open passenger divide. "He's my brother."

"You're Peña's sister?" Lyman said in disbelief.

"Well, I'll be a monkey's uncle!" the cabbie cried. "Your brother's been worried sick! He must have called you fifty times on the marathon ride down here."

"My cell phone is in my lost purse. Where'd you drop Alex? How long ago?" Claudia deposited Liberace on Lyman's lap and scooted out the taxi door.

"Fifteen minutes, max, at your apartment building," the driver answered.

Claudia knew Alex would search high and low. She wanted to find Seamus before Alex found her. "Please make sure Mayor

Fink's dog is taken to the animal hospital and Mr. Newlin gets back to the *Chronicle*." Claudia flashed a quick smile at Lyman. "I'll contact you later with the rest of the information."

"Huh? Where you going?" Lyman protested, adjusting his knees beneath the bandaged dog.

Liberace moaned.

Bella slid over to the far window.

"I have something to do." Claudia closed the cab door and hollered. "Go, hurry!" The taxi driver obeyed. Claudia jumped a snowdrift and sprinted back towards the subway station.

Simon followed close behind.

There was an unusually loud clap of thunder followed by an odd burst of colorful lightning. Claudia paused for a moment to watch. It reminded her of the 4th of July.

Seamus's transported-self stood on the bank of a large pond. He noticed turbulence beneath the bloodstained surface.

"Shoot the other nigger too," a man's voice yelled. "We don't need no witness."

A young black boy emerged from the water, panting and scrambling to keep afloat. A gruesome carcass popped up beside him.

The rifleman pulled his trigger.

A second bullet hit the dead man and showered the boy with another splatter of grey-matter.

Seamus's reactive mind-self felt the furious urge to leap, to fight, to rip the shooter to shreds. The tingle of transmogrification was becoming a pulsating burn raging through his veins. *Whatever you do don't change.* Seamus focused every ounce of his energy on something positive... *Claudia.* Her beautiful face held his anger at bay, for the moment…

The boy re-submerged from the stained water for a second, then sank again.

"I missed'm!" The shooter pointed. "Maybe he'll drown."

"Or maybe I'm gonna break his dern neck," the second man said, pulling up his pant legs and wading into the pond.

"I hear shooting!" a woman's voice screamed in the near distance. "TJ!"

A well-dressed man on horseback cantered into view. "Tom!"

Seamus thought he resembled a character from JOHNNY TREMAIN.

"Cease your fire," the man commanded. "Tom, where are you?"

Seamus's thought shifted to the boy. He found himself transported into another scene. He was now standing mid-water beneath the pond's surface, facing the drowning young Tom.

"TJ, I don't know if you can hear me," Seamus pleaded. "TJ, this is just a bad memory. You live. You grow-up. You steal my motorcycle."

The boy's eyes were wild and wide, but he stopped thrashing.

"TJ, fast forward to the part where you're saved," Seamus instructed. "There has to be happy ending here, somewhere."

222

The boy blinked.

Seamus and young TJ were now on the shore. Tom lay naked in his mother's cradling arms.

"My baby," she sobbed and rocked and kissed her son.

Seamus was struck by her exotic beauty, her rich coffee skin and hair, her fine regal features, and her impressive athletic physique. TJ had inherited his mother's biceps.

TJ opened his eyes and coughed. "Mama, sorry."

"He's alive! My baby is alive!" The jubilant mother showered her son with another barrage of kisses. "I love you. Oh, Tom, why you run off and scare yor mama?"

The grey-haired fair-skinned rider knelt beside her.

Seamus noticed that the man's distinguished clothing was now wet and soiled. The rider lifted TJ from his mother's arms and placed him on the horse. "Are you strong enough to hold on, boy?"

"Yes, Sir," TJ replied.

TJ's mother stood. She was as tall as the gentleman rider. She removed a shawl from her shoulders and placed it around her son's waist.

A gruff voice interrupted the tender moment. "Ah, Mr. Jefferson?" The gun-totting man lowered his head. His partner nudged him. "I mean, Sir," the killer stammered. "We didn't know the boy was yer nigger."

Thomas Jefferson, soon-to-be second president of the United States of America, mounted his horse and secured his arm around TJ. Young Tom leaned his head against the statesman's chest. "This boy is not my property," the statesman corrected. "He is my son."

TJ's eyes blinked.

Seamus and TJ were back in the twenty-first century.

Alex barreled out of the apartment building's double glass doors.

"Mr. Peña!" The ancient doorman scooted out of the Bomber's way and lost his balance. Freddy grabbed onto the awning pole and spun around.

Alex clutched the doorman by his coat before he swirled to the ground. "I'm so sorry," Alex cried. "Feel like I'm in a blind fog!"

"That's OK, Mr. Peña." Freddy righted himself with effort. "More important, did you find your sister?" Freddy asked. "She leave a note? Any clues?"

"Nothing," Alex groaned. "Doesn't look like Claudia returned home after her ride yesterday morning. Her cat definitely wasn't putting on a starving act." Alex held his head. "She's been gone since Saturday morning, Freddy."

"You better contact the police, Mr. Peña," Freddy, declared looking grave. "Better yet, you should go over to the police station yourself and file a missing person's report. They gonna think you're a prankster if you phone saying you're Alejandro Peña."

"Yeah, probably right," Alex agreed, the remaining color draining from his cheeks. "Call me a cab."

"I'm sorry Mr. Peña. It's early Sunday morning and it's a blizzard. I ain't seen a taxi since you pulled up here from Bean Town."

Alex punched the air. "Son of a—"

"Hold on there, Mr. Peña, I got a suggestion." The doorman took Alex by the arm and led him to the curb. "If you walk across the street you can catch the southbound M. The trains are always running. Go two stops to Park Place and the 20th police precinct is right there at the top of the exit stairs."

"The subway?" Alex protested. "But?"

"There ain't gonna be no autograph hounds on a day like this." Freddy coaxed Alex along. "It's the subway or run. And I don't think you wanna be breaking one a those zillion dollar limbs a yours slipping on a ice patch." Freddy removed a token from his pocket and pressed it into Alex's palm. "There ain't no present like time and your sister Claudia's might be running out."

Sergeant Gaffney stood on the subway platform and checked his wristwatch. The timer flashed. He tried his radio again. "This is Gaffney. Does anyone read? Over."

"Sarge," Seamus's voice crackled over the airwaves. "I'm with TJ. Over."

"Listen, Seamus, the trains are coming back on soon." Gaffney glanced at his watch again. "I'm at the Park Place station. Time's running out fast. Over."

"Sarge, we need to find the others. Start looking. Stay in touch. Over."

"10-4. Over and out."

Sergeant Gaffney secured his gun holster, climbed down the service ladder onto the subway tracks, and sprinted into the unknown.

"Where are we going, Miss Claudia?" Simon was grinning and having the time of his dead life.

Claudia removed a flashlight from her satchel, sat on the edge of the subway platform, and slid herself onto the tracks. "I need to catch up with Seamus." Claudia dusted off the seat of her pants. "When my brother realizes that I haven't been home he's going to freak and summon the cavalry. When they find me I'll probably end up with a bodyguard, and I'm not looking forward to that." Claudia pointed her beam towards the dimly lit tunnel. "Don't know what type of werewolf mission is going on down here, but I can't return home until I'm certain Seamus is OK."

"And you want me to say 'Benjamin Allen' three times?" Simon again practiced his lines.

"Right," Claudia replied. "We have work to—" Her sentence was interrupted by the faint sound of chanting. "Simon, do you hear that?"

"People singing."

"Hey, who's there?" Claudia shouted. She jogged along the passage in the direction of the vigorous voices. "Seamus? Sevlow? It's me, Claudia!"

"One, two, three, four, beelzebubbles have taken the store. Five, six, seven, eight, murder and mayhem we create. Nine, ten, eleven, twelve honor the Deep with a swing of our helve."

"I don't understand what they're talking about," Simon said.

"Me neither, but they're getting closer. And something *really* stinks again!" Claudia held her nose. Simon and Claudia turned the bend and found themselves face-to-face with the mayor and his house staff. Cook, gardener, maid, butler, and chauffeur, stood at rapt attention beside fake Fink, each one of them still holding the helve of their tool: spade, shovel, hoe, trowel, and gravy ladle. Claudia released her nose. "Mayor Fink! What are—" She didn't finish the question before the rim of a dirty shovel connected hard with her forehead, splitting it on impact and thrusting her backwards onto a pile of gravel between the subway rails.

"Miss Claudia!" Simon screamed.

Maid stepped forward and lifted her sharp-edged spade.

"She's as good as dead." Fake Fink raised his hand and prevented the second strike. "A train will be by soon enough. We must finish our job and close the portal before the werewolves find it."

Simon grabbed a handful of rocks and hurled them at the assailant. Gardner didn't appear to notice. The sinister sextet stepped over a motionless Claudia and disappeared beyond. "Miss Claudia," Simon cried, floating frantically above her critically injured body. "Please, Miss Claudia, please don't die!" A twist cap protruded from the sprawled satchel. Simon removed the bottle and splashed some water on Claudia's hemorrhaging gash. Diluted blood pooled between her parted lips.

"Mami," Claudia moaned. A red river ran down her chin, onto the collar of her white blouse. "Ma…"

"Your mother and father," Simon shrieked. "I have to find them!" His face was wrought with panic and uncertainty. "But I shouldn't leave Miss Claudia here alone." Time was running out fast, and the little child knew it. He disappeared.

Chapter 22

BETWIXT A DEEP AND A DARKSIDE

The beelzebubble belched the foreign object from its sucking grip. *Hmmm…* The rectangular zippered container was like no other item it had ever retrieved before. *What a score!* Previously the portal-guarding beelzebubble had sucked single shoes, keys, and chewed gum down the corridor from above, but it had never sucked something as remarkable as this. Beelzebubble could feel the negative energy, the angry emotion, and the toxic love oozing from every fiber of its four-sided find.

The beelzebubble knew it had to share the fascinating artifact, right away.

A supervisory meeting of the monstrous minds congregated in the depths of the Deep. Mickey's Communion picture floated in the darkness, all unseeing eyes upon it.

"Mama's boy," boss beelzebubble burped, scrutinizing the celluloid.

"Rotten to the core," a bulging beelzebubble belched. "And dead as a doornail."

"Still wallowing in limbo," a stinky seer noted. "But headed to the Darkside." The whole hole went hush.

"Bring me his willing soul!" boss beelzebubble burped. "He will be mine! Now!" An effervescing cheer erupted.

"I'll send word," the putrid portal guard replied. "At once."

Chapter 23

A RUMBLE IN THE TUNNELS

Alex checked his watch for the tenth time. Two excruciating minutes had passed. *Where's that train?* He shook his wrist and placed the sapphire crystal against his ear. *Still ticking.* Alex leaned his torso over the yellow caution line and scanned the dark tunnel. There was no sign of the M train. He resumed restless pacing along the subway platform.

The sound of gumshoe against gravel reverberated through the southbound corridor. It roused Alex out of his dire thought. "Hello?" Alex called, peering into the dimness. "Someone down there?" The crunching was getting closer.

"Sevlow?" came the out of breath response. "It's me… Gaffney." A jogger in NCPD blue trudged into view. He stopped underneath a light on the station wall and momentarily peered up at Alex. "You're not…" he panted, bending over, hands on hips. "I was hoping…"

"You're a police officer," Alex said, his spirits lifted for a brief moment. "I'm headed to the 20th precinct to file a report."

"Trains aren't running," Gaffney replied, a bit less winded. "But they'll be on soon. I have men down here to warn. Gotta go."

"Hold on, please," Alex implored. "My sister Claudia hasn't been home since yesterday morning. I'm out of my mind worried." Gaffney stopped short in his plodding tracks and stared at Alex. "Have you heard anything about a missing teen?"

"Holy smokes," the Sarge muttered, grabbing his head.

"You OK?"

Gaffney gave Alex a second, more careful, once-over. "Thought you looked familiar," he groaned. "You're Alejandro Peña."

"What do you know about my sister?" Alex said in a controlled panic. "Have you gotten any reports? Any calls? Do you know if she's alive?" The policeman seemed to be agonizing over his impending explanation. "Tell me!" Alex demanded. "Tell me what you know about Claudia!"

"You'd never believe a word of it." The officer let out a pained sigh.

"Try me." Alex was doing his best not to sound forceful.

"Your sister Claudia's been safely locked away in a tomb." Gaffney swallowed hard and hesitated. "Because, long story short, she's dating a hound... sorta... wolfish ... dog, but a great guy."

"*Lobo sueño*," Alex gasped. "He's real!"

"I don't understand Spanish, but yeah, Seamus is real and he's in trouble right now, so I've gotta go." The officer's radio hissed and crackled.

"Sarge, it's me again, Seamus. You read? Over."

Sarge removed the receiver from his pants pocket. He pressed the TALK button. "I read, Seamus. Over."

"That him?" Alex mouthed.

Gaffney nodded in the affirmative.

"Haven't found the others yet," Seamus relayed. "But TJ just remembered something about fireworks. Hear anything? Over."

"About fireworks? Negative. But I just ran into Alex Peña. Told him his sister's hidden from this mess, secure. Over."

"Claudia escaped," Seamus replied. "I saw her…" The radio began to buzz and hum and fade in and out. "…minutes ago…. dog…hurt… Over."

"Seamus?" Sergeant Gaffney banged the radio on his palm before trying to reconnect. "Seamus, you're breaking up. Do you read? Over." Silence.

"Claudia doesn't have a dog." Alex paced back and forth. "If she's down there, I'm coming with you to find her." He readied himself for a leap onto the subway tracks.

"Wait," the Sarge cautioned. "We're dealing with weird supernatural stuff."

"Thanks to my sister," Alex confessed. "I am all too familiar with weird and supernatural stuff."

"What about other impending danger?" Sarge offered another out. "You could be hurt. An injury might destroy your career."

Alex pushed up the sleeves of his leather jacket. "Nothing in this world is more important to me than my sister, Claudia."

"Can't argue with that." Sergeant Gaffney flashed a warm smile. "Just do me a favor. I'm a big Bomber's fan." He pointed. "Please use the service ladder."

Seamus slipped the silent radio back into his pants pocket without breaking his hurried stride. "Guess we're in a dead zone."

"Yeah, from Twilight Zone to Dead Zone." TJ adjusted the backpack slung over his bare shoulder. "Thanks again, man. Owe you one."

"You'd have done the same for me." Seamus was sure of it.

"So, Peña's down here looking for his sister," TJ remarked. "How'd he get back from Bean Town?"

"No idea. But I'm sure he's pissed," Seamus groaned. "I know I'd be."

"If Peña gives you any trouble I'll kick his ass." TJ cracked a playful grin. "Get turned into a werewolf and it's *un pour tous, tous pour un.*"

"Three Musketeers movie quote?" Seamus laughed. "D remember every line—"

A blood curdling scream cut Seamus's sentence short.

"Bet they've found the mayor and the portal." TJ broke into a sprint. "Time for Elvis to leave the building!"

"How do you best a beelzebubble?" Seamus asked, keeping stride.

"Take its human host to the brink of death," TJ said. He hurdled a cement block. "Like a rat on a sinking ship the beelzebubble will ditch a body it thinks is about to die."

"With no other open mind to enter," Seamus deduced. "They retreat."

"By Jove I think he's got it!" TJ cried. "Secure your thoughts. We're going in!"

Seamus and TJ bounded into a rumble in progress. Werewolf-forms Sevlow, Dragon, and Mighty Mouse were corralling the mayor and four of his tool-wielding house staffers beside the portal. The maid lay motionless behind Dragon.

"Well, look who's here," fake Fink taunted, motioning for his band of beelzebubbles to stop swinging. "It's bastard slave boy and his orphan sidekick. Still sad your unwed mommy didn't want to keep you, Seamus?" The hideous house staff roared with laughter.

Seamus felt his blood run hot and his pupils dilate. His body began to writhe and contort. Sevlow's human voice entered Seamus's transforming brain.

"Don't let them manipulate you."

Seamus held Claudia's face in his mind's eye as he repeated her name. His vision completely blurred and blanked for what seemed an instant. Lights out.

When Seamus came to he was on all furry fours, nose-to-nose with Cooke the cook and her careening ladle. Seamus took a whack to the temple. He countered with a left paw that sent the assailant tumbling backwards.

Sevlow leapt on the woman and seized her neck between his frothing fangs. Blood began to trickle from a shallow puncture beside her right ear.

Cooke shrieked.

Sevlow clenched.

A putrid pulsating bubble popped through the cook's nostril and hovered for a brief moment in front of the white werewolf's steely blue stare. The defeated beelzebubble retreated down the portal, back to the Deep. Sevlow lifted the cook onto his back and placed her beside the maid. Neither woman was conscious.

There was a faint rumble in the distance.

"Do-good werewolves have chased us back to the portal." The malicious mayor removed a soiled handkerchief from his pajama pocket and waved it in the air. "You win; we lose. The gods' great hounds leave the beelzebubbles with but one tiny victory, a mass suicide." Fake Fink and the others secured their filthy feet beneath a subway rail. "I hope the mayor's tragic death makes New City *explode* with sorrow," he cackled with maniacal glee.

Dragon and Benjamin, transfer the injured to a safe location.

Seamus heard Sevlow's urgent thought transmission. Dragon and Mighty Mouse acted at once. Seamus and TJ took their teammates' vacated places, crouched before the remaining beelzebubbles, fangs bared and ready for action.

"¡*Dios mio!*" someone shouted.

Seamus was about to thought-mention TJ's fireworks recollection when the unfamiliar voice distracted him. He turned his attention away from the cunning captives for a split second. *It's Peña and the Sarge!*

Gardner took advantage of the unguarded moment. He lunged forward.

"Duck!" Gaffney warned before hitting the deck.

The back of gardener's shovel whizzed past Seamus's snout and connected hard with Alex's left shoulder. THUNK! Instead of collapsing, Alex spun around and with his right hand snatched the shovel from the stunned beelzebubble's grasp. In a second, even more fluid movement, the Bomber gripped the tool helve like it was a Louisville slugger and swung with a vengeance. CRACK! Gardener flew past Seamus.

Homerun! thought Seamus.

Claudia's eyes opened. She lifted her hand to touch her forehead. It no longer throbbed or bled. She felt no scab or scar. Bright, warm, calming light bathed her body. Claudia sat up with ease and observed her serene surroundings. She was dressed in a perfectly fitting pink chiffon gown, and perched upon an ornate canopy bed in a floating bedroom. The enclosure had no walls. Claudia smiled as she canvassed the boudoir and the whiteness beyond. She wondered if the scene was real. Perhaps she had fallen asleep and entered a blissful dream. No matter. Claudia never wanted the encounter to end. She felt loved. She felt safe. She felt peaceful.

She felt a hand grab her ankle and yank her off the bed.

"Claudia!" Paz shouted at her dying daughter. "¡*No te duerma!*"

"Please, Claudia," her father pleaded. "Do not sleep. Your mami and I cannot continue to pull you back from the other side."

Simon shook a few drops of water onto Claudia's face.

She let out a soft moan.

"Good boy!" Paz cried. "Please, keep Claudia awake."

Salvador wrung his hands and hovered above his daughter's expiring body. "We must think! How do we summon help?"

"If only we could call the werewolves," Simon said. "They would help."

"*¡Eso es!* That is it!" Paz threw her arms around Simon.

"*¡Lobo sueño!*" Salvador knelt beside his daughter and whispered into her ear. "Claudia, if you can hear me, call to Seamus. He is your only hope. Enter your werewolf dreams, Claudia. Ask Seamus to save you. Go to him!"

Gardener was still out cold. Three down. Three remaining. The werewolf trio each had a beelzebubble in their sights.

Seamus's emerald eyes were fixed on Fink.

"Go ahead, orphan boy," the mayor goaded. "You've spent your whole life behaving recklessly. So go ahead, tear me to shreds. Murder me."

"Don't listen to him, Seamus," Sergeant Gaffney called from a safe distance. "Focus your thoughts on something positive."

Fury raged in Seamus's gut.

"Think about my sister," Alex shouted, holding his injured shoulder.

"Claudia's dead," fake Fink crowed. "The garbage man's scooping her pretty brains off the subway tracks as we speak."

"He's a liar!" Alex screamed.

Seamus's jaws clamped down on the tormenter's thigh.

The mayor cackled with delight.

Sevlow's words of caution were interrupted inside Seamus's head.

"Seamus," whispered a faint familiar voice. "Help me."

Claudia? Seamus released Fink's femur and looked up.

There she was, a bloodied battered sight to behold, in her dimming sphere of flickering luminescence.

"Save me, Seamus," Claudia begged. "I'm dying."

Rumble, Rumble, Rumble.

Seamus abandoned one fight for another.

Seamus followed the sweet scent of blood into an adjacent tunnel. He found Claudia. Her motionless body and blood-soaked hair were draped across the cold hard subway tracks. The gruesome sight wrenched Seamus to his undead core. He wanted to kill someone. *Stop! Stay focused. Claudia needs me.* Seamus talked himself back from the brink of rash madness. He nuzzled Claudia's neck. There was a weak pulse. Seamus maneuvered her inert body across his broad back.

Claudia's eyes opened for a brief second.

Seamus wished he could assure Claudia that everything would soon be all right. That he would carry her to safety and stay at her side until she was healed and strong and her perfect self again.

RUMBLE, RUMBLE, RUMBLE.

Seamus could see the lights of the oncoming train fast approaching. A leap to the subway platform would be no large feat for an agile werewolf. However, it was a near impossibility for a werewolf carrying a semiconscious slack rider. He had to try. Seamus lifted and extended his front paws. Claudia's limp body slid backwards.

RUMBLE, RUMBLE, RUMBLE.

Seamus shifted his haunches. Claudia slipped further. The speeding train was approaching. There was no time to secure his passenger and attempt a second jump. In an effort to shield Claudia from the impending strike, Seamus twisted his massive furry body around Claudia's in an engulfing half-moon hug. His jaws were positioned above the orb of her left breast. Seamus could hear her fading heart.

The conductor spotted a big black dog curled on the subway tracks. TOOT! He pulled the emergency break. TOOT!

The train was going too fast to stop. Seamus knew what he had to do—he plunged his razor-sharp fangs into Claudia's chest and ripped out her heart. Bone-crushing impact and a cacophony of frenzied cries ushered Seamus into oblivion.

Lights out.

Chapter 24

AN IMMODEST PROPOSAL

Seamus awoke in human form in a pool of thick red goo. He was groggy. He was disoriented. He tried to sit up until he realized Claudia's tattered torso was still pressed between his arms. Fear and panic gripped Seamus as he assessed the carnage he was clutching. Along with producing countless gashes and purple bruises, the speeding train had severed both of Claudia's legs and hands, and her left eye hung precariously from its smashed socket. Seamus didn't flinch at the sight. He was running on adrenaline. He moved aside what was left of Claudia's shredded riding blazer. Her extracted heart was still beating. Seamus cast his eyes to the heavens and breathed a grateful sigh of relief.

"Seamus," human-form Sevlow called from the subway platform above.

"She's not dead." Seamus was careful not to jostle Claudia. He held still and shifted his gaze. "Anyone get the number of that train?"

"Man, you scared the flying flip outa me!" TJ put his hand over his heart. "Now you're cracking jokes. You ain't right!"

Sevlow glided onto the tracks. "Allow me to examine her."

Seamus released Claudia's body to Sevlow. "I think she's turned."

The veteran werewolf inspected Claudia's pounding heart before pressing it back into the crushed cavity that was once her chest.

"I didn't have a choice." Seamus anticipated a reprimand.

"Of course you did," Sevlow remarked. "And you chose well. Your instincts were keen, excellent execution."

"Thank you, Sir," Seamus replied. "But how come she still looks like, like that?" The gruesome visual had begun to take hold. Seamus felt ill.

"In cases where the body has been badly damaged the initial progression from mortal to undead sometimes requires assistance." Sevlow popped Claudia's eye back into its ragged hollow.

Seamus lowered his head and looked away. "I heard screams before the train strike. Was anyone else hurt?"

Sevlow pointed a bloody finger towards the platform.

Seamus realized TJ was standing beside a big prone body. "Is that Peña?"

"He's alive," Sevlow assured. "Thanks to TJ."

"Big brother chased after you," TJ said. "I caught up with him on the northbound tracks just as the train was making its way into your side of the station. Peña was about to leap onto the rails when I tackled him. Guess I used a little too much force."

Alex moaned and stirred.

243

"He'll be coming to any minute." TJ knelt beside Alex. "I predict Peña's going to have one heck of a headache to go with his shovel shoulder."

"Seamus," Sevlow instructed. "Block Peña's view of his sister while I gather her limbs. She must be moved before the next train arrives."

Seamus positioned himself as directed. "What about Fink and the others?"

"Forced into an engineering booth. Dragon and Benjamin are standing guard." Sevlow lifted Claudia and placed her on the platform's concrete ledge. He set her feet and hands alongside their corresponding stumps.

Rumble, rumble, rumble.

Seamus was going to ask about the portal, until he noticed the blood puddle on the tracks. It was beginning to disappear. So was the scarlet wetness on his skin and clothing. Seamus turned his attention to Claudia. Her parts had reattached. Seamus hoisted himself onto the subway ledge. He sat beside Claudia and watched. Once the transformation began it was swift and steady.

Claudia stretched her perfectly refurbished body and opened her eyes. Two emerald green irises were staring back at her. "Oh, Seamus." Claudia yawned. She felt woozy, in a relaxing sort of way. "I had the craziest dream."

Seamus leaned forward for a kiss.

"No smoochy-face," TJ interrupted. "Our work's not done yet."

Sevlow knelt between Seamus and Claudia. " No time for a lengthy preface. Ms. Peña; you've been turned into a werewolf."

"What! I'll smell like a wet dog forever?" Claudia sprang up and sniffed herself. "Oh my gosh! I stink! But how could this be? Claudia patted her arms and legs looking for proof. "I feel fine. Nothing's broken."

"Do you have any recollections of the prior events?" Sevlow asked.

"I remember being hit in the head," Claudia said. "I was with Simon." She looked around for her little companion. He was nowhere to be seen.

"Simon?" Seamus repeated. "Who's he?"

"Benjamin's brother." Claudia didn't elaborate. "We ran into the mayor, then a man hit me with a shovel. After that, it's all a blank. Except for a strange dream."

"It appears the beelzebubbles left you for dead on the subway tracks," Sevlow explained. "Seamus gave you a new life, just in time."

"Wow! When this all sinks in I'm going to really freak out," Claudia said. "But at the moment I feel amazing, like I've been recharged." She didn't know how else to explain the warm tingling sensation surging through her body.

"Turning sorta feels like sucking in after eating a peppermint," Seamus said.

"Or sitting on the jet in a hot tub," TJ added. "Or—"

"No time for analogies," Sevlow interrupted. "I apologize for being brusque; however, now that the trains have resumed operation, we must vacate the station." Sevlow helped Claudia to her feet. "Werewolves work best behind the scenes."

Alex groaned and opened his eyes.

Claudia peered past Seamus. "My brother!" she cried. Her good vibrations were replaced by horrible dread. She rushed to Alex's side and wrapped her arms around him. "He's here too?"

"Yes, unfortunately, you're brother became involved in our ordeal," Sevlow explained. "He's been injured, but should fully recover."

"I hope I'm in my hotel room." Alex sat up. "I'm having a horrible nightmare. I didn't save my sister from being hit by a speeding train."

Claudia hugged her brother. "This is all my fault!"

"Back-from-the-dead dream sister is crushing my chest." Alex winced. "And she smells like a wet dog."

"Better get used to my strength and my stink," Claudia replied in teary relief. "I'm a werewolf." She loosened her grip, but kept hugging. "Oh, Alex. I would have never forgiven myself if something happened to you."

Alex stroked his sister's hair. "Don't cry." His voice cracked. "So it wasn't a nightmare, baby sister. I was so afraid I'd lost you."

"I'm OK, just undead." Claudia helped her brother to his feet.

"A train hit you." Alex examined his sister's face.

"Claudia would have been gone forever," Sevlow replied. "If —"

"I know," Alex interrupted. "Seamus—" Alex's sentence was also cut short, by the sound of applause.

"Just what the world needs," fake Fink mocked, with his clapping cohorts in tow. "Another manufactured hound of the gods."

A brindle werewolf escorted Fink and two still-possessed house staffers into the mix. Dragon rapidly resumed his human shape.

TJ and Seamus struck defensive poses.

"Sir, the beelzebubbles would like to offer a proposal." Dragon looked behind him, as if he were expecting someone else.

Fake Fink removed a rolled piece of glossy paper from his pajama pocket. "Pity Seamus showed his cowardice and abandoned the pack back at the portal."

Claudia saw Seamus's body tense, his pupils began to dilate.

Sevlow placed a firm hand on Seamus's shoulder.

Fake Fink unrolled the 4"x6" rectangle. "This just arrived from the Deep via messenger." He held up a worn photograph. "Anyone here know a recently dead guy named Mickey Stella?"

"Holy smokes!" A breathless man approached from behind. "I think I talked to his mother yesterday morning." Sergeant Gaffney trudged over to the growing group. "I'm outa breath."

RUMBLE, RUMBLE, RUMBLE.

Everyone on the platform paused.

A train entered the station. The doors slid opened. No one got off and no one got on. The doors slid closed. The train disappeared into the dark subway tunnel beyond. Rumble, rumble, rumble.

Fake Fink rolled his eyes. "As I was saying."

"I know who Mickey Stella is." Claudia put a hand on hip. "He's a coldhearted murderer, just like you and your vicious smelly bubble pals." She surveyed the trio. "Which one of you hit me with a shovel?"

"I knocked out shovel-guy," Alex boasted. "He whacked me too."

"State your proposal," Sevlow said without a hint of sentiment.

"In exchange for Mickey's willing soul," fake Fink offered. "We will return to the Deep without further harm to the mayor and his staff, and we won't return."

"The duration of your proposed armistice?" Sevlow inquired.

"Sir," TJ interjected. "You're not considering his immodest proposal. We've got them beat. It's three beelzebubbles against the four of us."

"Five of us," Claudia corrected.

"I agree we fight. Don't trust him." Seamus was itching to turn.

"Diplomacy is the art of lying for one's country," Dragon added.

Sevlow held up his hand for his pack to silence. "How long?"

"We will stay out of New City until the next election," fake Fink bargained.

"A decade," Sevlow countered.

"We have a deal. In exchange for Mickey Stella's willing soul, beelzebubbles will refrain from creating crime waves, SARS scares, sanitation strikes, and springtime snowstorms for the next ten years."

"Oh, please," Claudia scoffed. "I just saw him cross his fingers."

249

Fake Fink shook his head. "That new one's going to be trouble."

"If this Mickey you speak of agrees to choose the Deep over his destiny in the Darkside," Sevlow replied. "Then the hounds accept your proposal."

Fake Fink held up his left hand. "Mickey's Darkside soul in exchange for ten years of letting New Citiers cause their own problems, Deep's honor."

"What's the difference?" Seamus asked. "Aren't the Deep and the Darkside both lousy places to end up?"

"I believe 'lousy' is a subjective word," the malevolent mayor replied. "There's a distinct difference between the Deep and the Darkside. On the Darkside there is nothing. No light, no happiness, no contact with others forever. In the Deep, rotten souls are put to work. Acquiring a willing rotten soul not only gives energy to the beelzebubble who brought it aboard, but its associates benefit as well—think network marketing from Hell."

Seamus shook his head. "Mickey's a big fat bully. Why would he agree to work, if he can do nothing for an eternity?"

"Because ten years of no bad stuff in New City would make my mama happy," a man's voice whined from above. "And making my mama happy and proud is something I wanna do while I still got the chance."

"It's Mickey's ghost!" Claudia pointed at the dark blob hovering above Fink. "Does anyone else see or hear him?"

There was a unanimous chorus of "no".

"Get used to it," Alex chimed. "Claudia speaks to the dead."

"They speak to me," Claudia corrected. "Mickey said he agrees to go to the Deep because he wants to make his mother proud. *And* Mickey wants me to tell authorities about the four people buried in his vegetable garden so their limbo souls can be released to heaven," she added.

"Hey! I didn't say nothing about that," Mickey protested.

Claudia felt a heightened sense of empowerment. She glared at the gray ghost.

"Oh, go ahead," grumbled Mickey. "Tell their families whatever you want."

"Then it's a deal," Claudia confirmed.

"Yes!" fake Fink cheered. "I'll get wicked points for recruiting a mama's boy who makes a sacrifice coupled with a good deed!"

POP! Three brown beelzebubbles exited the bottoms of their human hosts. The cataleptic bodies collapsed.

A putrid pulsating fog engulfed Mickey's nearly dark spirit and sped away.

"They're headed back to the Deep with Mickey," Claudia announced.

"Sir, I can't believe you let them go without a fight." Seamus shook his head. "We could have beaten them. Fink deserved it."

"There's more than one way to conquer evil." Sevlow checked his watch. "Fink was an innocent pawn in the beelzebubbles' game. His body couldn't have taken much more abuse." Sevlow turned towards Dragon and counted. "7-6-5-4…"

Dragon pulled a remote detonator from his pocket.

"3-2-1," finished Sevlow.

Dragon hit the button. CLICK. There was an explosion followed by a rapid succession of BANGs and POPs and BOOMs. Colorful bursts of cascading light filled the subway tunnel.

"What was that?" Claudia peered over the platform into the illuminated tunnel.

"The portal is no more." Dragon grinned. "Blown to smithereens."

"The beelzebubbles had planned to blow up the Washington Tunnel during tomorrow morning's rush hour," Sevlow said. "So we altered their plans."

"The most traveled commuter passage in New City," Sarge said in horror.

"The Arbor Day Parade," Seamus added. "The streets around Midtown Gardens would have been full of early spectators, most of them school children. If the tunnel collapsed, the streets above would have fallen. Hundreds, maybe thousands of innocent people would have been killed."

"That old tunnel is so decayed, a sparkler and a stiff wind could have taken it down," TJ commented. "No wonder they picked that target."

"How'd you figure out their plot?" Alex asked.

"Werewolves have a keen sense of smell." Sevlow grinned. "And Fink's pyrotechnic placement was quite shoddy."

"The beelzebubbles were headed back to the Washington Tunnel with more fireworks when Sevlow, Mighty Mouse, and I cornered them," Dragon said.

"He had no intention of making a fair deal," Seamus remarked. "And you knew it all along, Sir."

"Seamus, the years alone have taught you how to fight on the behalf of others," Sevlow said. "Now you will learn when not to. Warfare and reason are equally important werewolf skills."

"Sevlow had me disable the timer and reprogram the detonator. Then he and Mighty Mouse moved the fireworks to the portal," Dragon explained. "But one of the rockets shot out of a subway grate during transport."

Claudia remembered the loud thunder and weird lightning.

Seamus congratulated Sevlow. "You gave up nothing in the deal and won."

"It's called werewolf diplomacy." Sevlow smiled. "The werewolves' preferred route when innocent mortal lives are at stake."

"It's over, just like that?" Sarge sounded relieved and disappointed.

"We are not yet finished with our mission." Sevlow gave the orders. "Dragon, TJ, return to the portal and make sure it's secured."

TJ whispered to Seamus, "That means we leave our scent markings, if you know what I mean."

"Seamus, Sergeant Gaffney, call an ambulance for the mayor and his staff, and then alert the Transportation Department that the Washington Tunnel is on the verge of collapse and should be closed at once."

"How are we going to explain all this?" Gaffney asked.

"Don't worry," Claudia answered. "I have a story concocted and a contact at the *Chronicle* to tell it. When Lyman Newlin is done reporting, you and Seamus should be awarded another medal of honor."

Seamus raised an eyebrow. "You know Lyman Newlin?"

"Watch out guys," Alex warned. "My sister likes to take charge."

"Good," TJ said. "Let's put her in charge of cleaning up the wolf den."

Those who'd seen the den howled with laughter.

"Ha-ha," Claudia nudged Seamus. "You're supposed to be on my side."

"The lost boy pack is going co-ed," Dragon observed. "I'm predicting Claudia will be as valuable an addition as Seamus."

"Thanks, Dragon." Seamus took Claudia's hand. "She'll be our Wendy."

"More like Tinker Bell." Claudia gazed into Seamus's eyes and recited a line from her favorite childhood novel. "You know that place between sleep and awake, the place where you can still remember dreaming? That's where I'll always love you."

"Ah, speaking of characters," TJ interjected. "Where's Mighty Mouse?"

"I asked him to check on the other staffers and then meet up with us." Dragon checked his watch. "He should be here by now."

"Dragon." Seamus pointed. "There's a book on the ground by your foot."

Dragon picked it up and read the title, "IL LUPO APPASSIONATO."

"It means the passionate wolf," Claudia translated. She smiled at Sevlow.

"Ms. Peña," Sevlow removed his book from the ground and flashed Claudia a knowing grin. "Why don't you tell everyone what happened to Benjamin."

"Benjamin is with his brother," Claudia said. "Simon called Benjamin home."

Chapter 25

EXTRA, EXTRA

Serial Killer on Murderous Kidnapping Rampage
Mayor Fink and Others Saved
By Lyman Newlin

New City, NY—Honorable Mayor Ed Fink and five of his staff members were drugged and kidnapped this weekend by an apparent serial killer. Bomber Alejandro Peña's sister was also kidnapped, but managed to escape unharmed. In addition, Ms. Peña is responsible for the fortuitous rescue of Mayor Fink's injured dog, Liberace.

Other victims were not as lucky. Four decomposed bodies were found buried in a residential vegetable garden in Sicily Town. Heroic citizen Mickey Stella, who led police to the serial killer and the bodies, also died. An anonymous witness saw Mr. Stella and the unnamed serial killer plunge into a subway sinkhole beneath Midtown Gardens Park. Neither body has been recovered.

"I remember a foul odor, which I mistakenly blamed on my loyal dog," said the mayor from his hospital bed at NC General, where he's stable, recovering from injuries. "I ingested the odorous substance, which was probably a form of knock-out gas."

Sergeant Ignatius Gaffney and Patrolman Seamus Sullivan were first on the scene. Sergeant Gaffney granted an exclusive interview. "On Saturday morning I answered a phone call from a concerned widow and mother, Mrs. Clarabella Stella. It triggered my suspicions that a situation was developing," said the sergeant, who is approaching his thirtieth year of exemplary service to the NCPD. "Mrs. Stella reported that her upstanding son Mickey did not return home after he met an unnamed business acquaintance the night before. It's customary to wait 48 hours before a missing person report can be filed, and Mrs. Stella politely agreed to adhere to procedure. However, her passionate call weighed heavily on my mind. I decided to personally investigate."

As the weekend progressed, there were more unusual developments.

"I received word that someone pretending to be Mayor Fink had requested that M and G train service be halted," said Sergeant Gaffney. "It was the big break. I sent Officer Sullivan to investigate the subway tunnels while I pieced together our other mounting leads. That's when Patrolman Sullivan found the huge crack in the Washington Tunnel wall." *continued on page 9A*

continued on page 9A

Alejandro Peña on Ten-Day Disabled List

By Lyman Newlin (filling in for Mike Le Pico)

New City, NY—A family emergency summoned Bomber Alejandro Peña back to New City Sunday morning from the team's snowed-out series in Bean Town. Peña was injured when he slid on patch of ice while making his way across Midtown Gardens Park during Sunday's blizzard. "My head and left shoulder hit the corner of a metal park bench after I slipped and fell," said Peña.

The team physician assured fans at this morning's press conference that the star Bomber would be ready for next week's sold-out series against the Pirates. *continued on page 24D*

continued on page 24D

TRAFFIC ALERT

The New City Department of Transportation announced on Sunday that the Washington Tunnel has been closed for extensive emergency repairs. Critical cracks were discovered in the subterraneous walls of the seventy-five year old structure. Commuters are asked to take the Midtown Garden's thoroughfare to the Heehawken ferry until the tunnel reopens. Additional bus service will also be made available during heavy traffic hours. *continued on page 3C*

continued on page 3C

Lyman Newlin to be Honored by Crime Reporter's Guild
By Namyl Nilwen

New City, NY—Veteran police reporter and investigative ace, Lyman Newlin, will be honored at the 21st annual Crime Reporter's Guild gathering being held over Memorial Day weekend in New City. "It's truly a privilege," said Mr. Newlin from his corner windowed office at the *Chronicle. continued on page 11B*

continued on page 11B

Mayor Fink Proposes Parcel Be Named in Honor of Fallen Hero
By Lyman Newlin

259

New City, NY—Mayor Fink established today that a portion of Sicily Town Park will be renamed Mickey Stella Garden in honor of the fallen hero whose life was tragically ended last weekend in the serial killer rampage. According to Mickey's mother, the lovely Clarabella Stella, her son was an avid gardener. "Mickey had a green thumb," she tenderly recalled. "He grew the sweetest peppers. They were the size of grapefruits."

A private fund has been established to turn the parcel into a community cooperative vegetable garden. Bomber Alejandro Peña has pledged a generous contribution to the horticultural endeavor.

Philanthropic Organizations to be Honored
By Lyman Newlin

New City, NY—St. Guinefort's Home for Orphaned and Troubled Boys will be awarded a scholarship by the Alejandro Peña Foundation at a charity dinner on Saturday night. Mayor Fink will host the star-studded event honoring local philanthropic organizations that have made a positive difference in New City. *continued on page 5A*

PEOPLE PAGE
Celebrated newspaper columnist Lyman Newlin was spotted dining at trendy Bacigaloop Café with a mature unnamed woman dressed in black. Witnesses say a young female admirer approached their secluded table and requested the reporter's

autograph. The fan was then physically and verbally assaulted by Mr. Newlin's date. Police had to be called to the scene.

Chapter 26

PINK MOON RISING

There was a vacant seat between Alex and Seamus at the head round table for ten. Seamus was decked out in his NCPD dress blues and sporting a new shiny gold medal for valor in the line of duty. He should have been socializing with his mates, but instead he stared at the reception hall entryway and fiddled with his fork. *Where is she?*

Claudia was late for the honorarium dinner. She'd missed the salad course and her pallet cleansing mango sorbet was presently up for grabs. Dragon and TJ argued the distinction between sherbet and sorbet while reaching across Seamus to dig their spoons into the frozen mound in a beveled bowl, in front of the only unoccupied chair.

"The difference is milk," TJ said. "Sherbet has milk and sorbet doesn't."

"They're same thing," Dragon insisted, slurping the remaining orangey puddle from the bottom of the glass bowl. "One word is English and the other is French. If we were in Italy, it would be called *gelato*."

"Yeah? If we were in Spain you'd be called *el slobo*," TJ teased. "Liberace has better table manners."

"Woof!" Liberace was seated beside Mayor Fink. His Honor's best friend sported a bow tie print bandana, a body wrap, and a well-autographed leg cast. Mayor Fink scratched the bandage on his forehead and surveyed TJ's outfit. "Your dress jacket, waistcoat, and ruffled shirt are perfect replicas of formal Federalist wear."

"Authentic Federalist formalwear," TJ corrected, brushing his brass-buttoned lapels. "Belonged to my father. My mom tailored it for me before I left home."

"Clothes don't make the man," Dragon noted, pushing up the sleeves of his black and white tuxedo-printed t-shirt. "But they make a lot of laundry."

Fink started to reply, but instead buttered a piece of a roll and fed it to his hound. "How's that shoulder?" he asked Alex. "Bet you're glad to be getting off the disabled list next week. Down time must have been grueling for an athlete like you."

"My shoulder feels 100% and I'm looking forward to being in the line-up again." Alex flexed his arm and placed it around the woman beside him. "I *have* managed to keep myself occupied while on the DH."

Violet, the bodacious purple-haired woman seated between Alex and the Sergeant Gaffney giggled. Her sequined halter-top nearly malfunctioned with each titter.

Sergeant Gaffney closed his eyes, but not right away.

"Is your sister typically late for engagements?" Fink asked when the awkward moment of pretending not to gawk had passed. "Perhaps you can present the scholarship to Fr. Benedict instead?" He turned to the padre seated to his right. "Would that be alright with you, Father?"

"St. Guinefort's boys are quite grateful, whomever presents the gift." The spectacled headmaster replied.

Seamus observed how much older Sevlow looked in his priestly costume.

"Claudia will be here in time for the award ceremony," Alex assured. "I sent the limo driver back for her."

Seamus glanced at his watch. "Moonrise is at 2035," he noted aloud.

"2035 is the same as 8:35 PM." Fink did the conversion. "Is the term moonrise interchangeable with sunset?"

"Not exactly," the headmaster replied. "The interval between sunset and moonrise varies. When there is a full moon, like tonight, the lapse is brief."

"About fifteen minutes," Seamus said, eyes still fixed on the doorway.

"Native Americans call the April full moon the pink moon," TJ noted.

"Not to be confused with June's strawberry full moon," Dragon added.

"Your former students are very knowledgeable, Fr. Benedict," the mayor said through an approving nod. "Astronomy must be a mandatory course at St. Guinefort's."

"Our curriculum is quite varied," the padre said through an elusive grin.

"Excuse me." Seamus stood and pushed in his chair. "I need to go check on something." He headed for the entryway as his target made her way into the room.

Claudia was a vision of elegant beauty, dressed in a flawlessly fitted pink chiffon cocktail dress, her chocolate hair swept back in a sophisticated updo. His pupils dilated and his heart raced. Seamus wished they were alone.

"Seamus," Claudia called above the mealtime chatter.

He hurried to greet her before anyone else had the chance to notice Claudia had arrived.

"Sorry I'm late. I made a few last minute edits to my speech. Miss me?"

"You look totally incredible," Seamus said. "And you always will."

"So will you," Claudia replied, stroking Seamus's close-shaved cheek. "I can't believe we're eternally seventeen."

"Eternity's a long time." Seamus was staring hard, memorizing every beautiful inch of her perfect face.

"At least werewolves can change clothes and hairstyles," Claudia said. "We need to stay young *and* fashionable"

Seamus took a step back and admired Claudia's dress. "You look gorgeous."

"It reminds me of a chiffon gown I wore in a dream," Claudia said. "When I died." Seamus leaned forward for a kiss. "Don't smudge my lipstick." Claudia placed her lips a hair's distance from Seamus's puckered mouth.

Seamus rolled his eyes and laughed. "Guess I can't touch your hair? And you wouldn't let your date pick you up for the big event, either."

"Hey, it's an important night for me," Claudia reminded. "Fear of wind and helmet head is why I declined your offer." She took Seamus's hand.

"So, you think you'll sprout salon-finished fur?" Seamus lead Claudia to the table of honor.

"Ms. Peña." Sevlow stood.

"Hi, Sir," Claudia replied in a cheerful familiar tone before addressing the others. "Mayor Fink, Dragon, TJ, Sergeant Gaffney, Violet, Alex. Forgive me for being late."

"Woof!"

"And you too, Liberace."

Seamus pulled out Claudia's chair, and seated himself beside her.

"You've met Fr. Benedict and his former students before?" Mayor Fink sounded surprised. "Not before the selection process?"

"Not before. We met recently," Claudia assured. "I was recruited after the scholarship school was selected, and after my kidnapping ordeal." Claudia squeezed Seamus's hand.

"Fr. Benedict hosts a sort of club," Seamus explained. "The focus is on doing good deeds, helping those in need. Tonight is her official induction."

"I'd be interested to see your group in action," Fink said.

"Invite Liberace and me to a meeting sometime."

"Beelzebubble," Dragon mumbled.

"Pack," TJ couched.

"Pardon me?" The mayor appeared confused.

"Then you must pack," Sevlow said. "Our charity work takes us many places."

"Hey! Who ate my sorbet?" Claudia examined her empty bowl.

TJ and Dragon pointed at Liberace.

A woman with a clipboard approached the table. "It stinks like wet dog around here," she said to herself, loud enough for all to hear. Fink placed a protective hand on Liberace and spun around in his chair. She caught sight of the mayor's defensive grimace. "Ah, pardon me, Mayor Fink, it's time for your speech and then the first presentation."

The mayor stood slowly and reached for the walking cane that was leaning behind his chair. Seamus remembered the thigh chomping. He felt a twinge of regret.

Claudia leaned over and whispered to Alex. "*Los padres* told me to remind you that the kitchen is off-limits." She cleared her throat and glanced at Violet. "And don't tell me being injured made you work up an appetite."

Alex flashed a Cheshire grin.

Sevlow peered at his timepiece.

"Sir, good thing you're up first." Seamus also checked his watch. "Hope the mayor doesn't care if some of us skip out early."

"Yeah," TJ tugged at his collar. "I'm starting to get a little hairy."

Sergeant Gaffney made a *shhh* signal and pointed a finger at Violet.

"Welcome, ladies and gentlemen to the fourth annual N Philanthropy Charity Dinner," Fink's voice boomed across the PA system. "This year the committee has decided to structure the evening a little differently. We will be presenting awards between courses, to help you digest."

"To hold us hungry captives," Seamus whispered.

"Do not fear; your main course will be served shortly. But first, it is my great pleasure to introduce New City's newest resident philanthropist, a man who in this baseball town, and most others, is so well-known he needs no lengthy introduction— Alejandro Peña, would you please stand?"

There was a huge round of applause. Alex stood and waved. Seamus noticed that the half a billion-dollar Bomber looked embarrassed. *So much for tabloids and first impressions.* Claudia squeezed Seamus's hand and smiled at her brother. Dragon and TJ gave Alex two thumbs up. Seamus surveyed the smiling, supportive table. *Family.* He finally had one.

"Tonight," Fink continued, after the Alex ovation was through. "I'd like to speak to you about the true meaning of charity. Genuine charity comes from a place in the heart of the giver. A place that yearns to make a difference in the world, no matter how slight that difference may appear to others. I am reminded of a story…"

Liberace whimpered. Dragon nudged TJ. TJ nudged Seamus. Seamus gave Claudia raised eyebrows.

"I think we're in for marathon speech." Seamus adjusted his seat.

"What do you want me to do?" Claudia asked in a hushed tone. "Run up there and grab his microphone?"

Seamus nodded "yes". So did the rest of the table. "We've got fifty minutes until moonrise. Either you take charge of this situation or—"

"Or I'm gonna munch on something besides stale dinner rolls," TJ warned. "This room's full of crooked politicians and greedy businessmen—a feast."

"And that brings me to my next story." Mayor Fink took a quick sip of water. "Back when I was in college there was a professor whom always took the time…"

Claudia looked to Sevlow for approval. The leader gave the go-ahead signal. Claudia took a deep breath, removed an envelope from her purse, and stood.

"He told us to cross the munificent threshold from charity to philanthropy requires not only an astute dedication to cause, but also the utmost conviction of one's…"

Claudia walked down the center isle and approached the podium. People began to comment to one another in hushed tones. Claudia stepped up beside Mayor Fink onto the raised platform.

His Honor's story came to an abrupt halt. "Ms. Peña?"

"Your talk so inspired me. I couldn't resist joining you here on stage." Claudia removed the microphone from bewildered Fink's hand, slid in front of the Mayor, and usurped the podium. "I once thought of New City as a cold unwelcoming metropolis, until my big brother joined the Bombers."

Mayor Fink stepped back without protest.

"Our move forced me to look at this town through different eyes, the eyes of an insider. Today, I am proud to call myself a New Citier. Because I've seen firsthand the goodness, the kindness, and the hope so many people here have to offer. They are New City's unsung heroes, heroes who work away from the limelight, heroes who work to make lives of others better, safer, and more promising. They are the stars who brighten the way of others less fortunate. One such quiet hero is Fr. X. Francis Benedict, headmaster of St. Guinefort's Home for Orphaned and Troubled Boys." Claudia gestured towards Sevlow. "Would you please come up here and join me, Sir?"

The head table erupted in cheers. Sevlow walked down the isle and approached the podium. Claudia took Sevlow's hand and guided him beside her.

"Since choosing St. Guinefort's as the recipient of this year's Alejandro Peña Scholarship Award, I have had the honor of seeing the headmaster in action with his boys." She paused. "And he is most inspiring. Fr. Benedict embodies the true meaning of leader. He is neither arrogant nor rude; he does not insist on his own way; he is neither irritable nor resentful; he does not rejoice at wrong, but instead he delights in the right and seeks the light."

Seamus could tell that stoic Sevlow had not anticipated Claudia's tribute speech. Seamus had before never seen him blush.

"Fr. Benedict, I am proud to call myself a member of your team." Claudia handed him the envelope. "It is with much respect and gratitude that I present to you this check, for your boys. May it benefit them for an eternity."

Sevlow stared at the gift. "Ms. Peña," he replied. "This, I don't know to say."

"My brother thought perhaps your school could use a scholarship fund, and a little something for your reserves." Claudia looked into the audience at Seamus. "Your boys deserve every opportunity to grow up to be worthy men."

The lost boys led the ovation. Seamus held up his arm and pointed at his watch.

Claudia raised her voice above the clapping. "And that concludes the first part of tonight's presentations," she speed-spoke. "Thank you, Mayor Fink." Claudia returned the microphone to His Honor and hurried off the stage with Sevlow.

"Well." Fink resumed his position at the podium. "That was quite a moving…" He paused to blow his nose. "It reminds me of a story I once heard. Told to me by a former Tibetan monk while we traveled aboard a yak through the snowy mountains of…"

Claudia rushed back to the table. "I'm starting to feel that sort of weird and tingling peppermint sensation," she said, touching her forehead.

"You were wonderful up there." Alex hugged his sister.

Sevlow reached out his hand, "Alex, your generous donation."

"No need, Sir," Alex interrupted. "The debt I owe you for Claudia is more than I could ever fully repay."

"Can we take a warm and fuzzy rain check here?" TJ begged. "I gotta go—now!"

"Sarge," Seamus asked. "Who's covering my park patrol shift?"

Gaffney shrugged and grinned, "See you in Midtown Gardens after the dinner. I'll bring the donuts."

Seamus and Claudia ran through the riding paths and reached the lake first.

An enormous pink moon filled the sky and reflected across the still water's mirror surface. Its light turned the budding spring trees into a forest of cotton candy.

Claudia took in the scene. "I can't remember the night looking more incredible."

Seamus wrapped Claudia in his arms. "You're my dream come true."

"I'm the one with the werewolf dreams, remember?"

"OK, so mine were more like fantasies." Seamus surveyed their lunar backdrop. "In less than a minute moonrise will be complete."

Claudia ran her fingers through Seamus's wavy black hair. "Wonder what would happen if we turned during a kiss? Would we awaken as werewolves, still locked in each other's arms?"

"If you're giving me permission to smudge your lipstick, there's only one way to find out." Seamus closed his emerald eyes, pressed his lips against Claudia's warm soft mouth, and let the full pink moon take them away.

Lights out.

www.ingramcontent.com/pod-product-compliance
Lightning Source LLC
Chambersburg PA
CBHW071129170626
46809CB00002B/546